D0461476

ALSO BY MATTHEW BETLEY

Overwatch

Oath Of Honor

Field Of Valor

Rules Of War

AMIRA

A Logan West Universe Novella

By Matthew Betley

For the readers who've kept Logan West alive
and kept me going, this one's for you.

Prologue

Smack!

Amira Cerone's pale blue gunslinger eyes fluttered open, and her heart raced with panic as she looked around the room in confusion. Her mouth was dry, but her body re-routed her attention to the wave of nausea that rolled upwards from the pit of her stomach. She felt the room spin, and she closed her eyes to fight the dizziness. On the verge of throwing up, she inhaled deeply until the sharp edge of nausea subsided. *That's one small relief.* But then her touch sense kicked into overdrive, which was when she realized her arms were bound behind her. *What the hell is going on?* she thought as her eyes flew open a second time to assess her situation.

Two dark-skinned people stood before her, calmly studying her actions. A man, the one who'd struck her, stared at her, smiling in a cold way that unnerved her more than the bindings on her wrists. She estimated his height at just under six feet, but he weighed no more than one hundred and seventy pounds, and that was giving him the benefit of the doubt. His light gray suit worn over a white shirt with a deep blue tie hung from his frame, accentuating his lankiness. His face was all angles, as if carved from granite until nothing was left but gashes for his eyes, nose, and mouth. His head was shaved in a buzz-cut, the black hair cut to less than a quarter of an inch as if it were his first day at boot camp. The austere visage was completed by brown eyes that mimicked the coldness of his smile. Had she passed him on the street, she

5

would've thought he was an unhappy accountant, a man who felt discontent in any profession.

"Tell her," the woman behind him said in an African accent. "Tell her, now."

Amira's glance shifted, and she studied the woman who'd spoken, her training powering back up with every new moment of consciousness. She was at least a half foot shorter than her partner, but unlike he, the woman wore a dark suit that highlighted her amazing physique in all the right places. With thick black hair, braided and tied into a ponytail, her features were softer than the man's, high cheekbones and full lips that invited lustful attention. But unlike the man, there was no smile. Only contempt, contempt that couldn't be disguised through feigned politeness. *Wonderful. A dynamic duo. John would love this,* her mind snapped, fixing on the man who'd become the love of her life, John Quick. *No time for distractions. Whatever this is, it isn't good. Focus, stay calm, and assess your surroundings.*

Amira glanced around and realized she was in a hotel room. Taupe drapes were drawn across the windows to her left. She was bound to a sturdy chair, which had been positioned between two queen-size beds, their luxurious white comforters still folded back crisply as if the cleaning crew had departed moments ago. The entire room was decorated in shades of tan and brown, tastefully and with purpose. A flat-screen TV stood on a dresser behind the woman, and a doorway to the right of the dresser led to another room. To the right of the door was the typical bathroom area in an

6

alcove that Amira assumed led to a bathroom behind the wall to her right. *Okay. I'm in some kind of suite. But what hotel? If I can figure that out, I'll be ahead of the game.*

"You're in the Gaylord National Hotel in a suite on the top floor," the man said politely, as if he were a concierge providing information to a guest who'd just arrived in the lobby.

The Gaylord? That meant the main room had at least one balcony that overlooked the massive glass cathedral-style atrium and the multi-tiered indoor lobby that was more like a shopping village with its abundant restaurants, stores, and coffee shops.

Amira brought her gaze back to the man, and her mind attempted to shake off the effects of whatever drug they'd used on her. *This isn't good. He doesn't care that you know. That means he doesn't think you're getting out of this room, ever.*

"Who are you?" Amira asked, her speech slightly slurred.

"It's the effect of the Rohypnol. I'm sorry about the dosage, but we had to get it just right, enough to impair you after you left the restaurant but not kill you or knock you out for hours. It made you just vulnerable enough once you reached the parking garage. The combination of chloroform from the rag and the drug I'm sure isn't pleasant, but it beat the alternative. Trust me," the man said, the cold smile broader.

"Which was?"

"Killing you right away," the man said with no emotion. *Just the facts, ma'am. Just the facts.* The words from the old police show hammered other images into her head, her father, a retired DC homicide detective, dying in her arms more than ten months ago. The sudden sucker punch of grief slammed into her gut, but she fought it off as she'd been doing since the day of his murder, building her defenses a little stronger with each random emotional attack. *Focus, Amira,* Nick Cerone's voice whispered inside her head. *Yes, Daddy,* she thought, love and anguish mixed in her mind. She shut the feelings down and breathed as each inhalation calmed her racing thoughts.

"Sounds like I'm a lucky girl," Amira replied, a note of resistance and sarcasm in her voice.

The woman moved forward so quickly Amira barely had time to register it before she felt the open hand twist her head to the left from the force of the blow. *She's fast. Not as fast as you, but still quick.*

"Please," the man said, chastising the woman. "No more. We can't have any marks on her body."

The way he referred to her "body" unnerved her, as if she were already dead and on display on a medical examiner's table. "Ms. Cerone, you can call me Samuel, and this is Nafisa, but it's irrelevant. As I'm sure you already figured out, this will be your final resting place, at least until the police discover your body. But until that time comes, I have no plans to torture or interrogate you. Nafisa, on the other hand, if I were to leave you to her, she would carve you apart, piece by piece, I believe, taking her time with each cut."

Amira's cheek throbbed, but she looked defiantly at Nafisa. "Do I know you? If so, I don't recall, and I never forget a face. *Ever.*"

Nafisa lurched forward, snarling and seething with hatred, but Samuel's arm shot out and blocked her progress before she could reach Amira. Samuel said something sharply in his native tongue, and Nafisa turned and exited the room.

Must have been good, whatever I did. Wait a second. What language was that?

"Since we're apparently all friends here already, can you answer me one simple question?"

Samuel's eyes raised in expectation. "Very well. Ask."

"What language was that? As I'm sure know, I'm half Ethiopian, and I know my African dialects, but the drug you used must be playing tricks on me, because I couldn't identify that one."

Samuel nodded his head slightly, exhaling quickly as if in agreement with her. "It's Dinka," he responded crisply, and waited for her to process the information.

Dinka? Amira had been to Africa on multiple missions, the most recent one nearly a year and a half ago when she'd been sent under cover as a USAID worker in Khartoum, where she'd met and partnered with Logan West, John Quick, and Cole Matthews, the three men with whom she'd later formed Task Force Ares. But before that fateful encounter, she'd been sent to southern Sudan, activated as a member of CIA's LEGION program, a female assassin and army of one. *Oh no. It can't be.*

9

Her features must've have given her away, because Samuel smiled at her self-realization. Before he could speak, there was a light knock on the door in the main room of the suite, and Samuel abruptly turned and walked away.

Amira's mind raced as she struggled to determine what the connection was with the mission in southern Sudan, although for Nafisa, she feared she already knew. *I killed someone she loved. As John would say with a corny wisecrack, this is going from bad to CATS, fast.* She smiled inwardly, encouraged that the voice of her lover and fellow warrior was always with her. *But bad musical movies aside, you have to focus, or you won't get out of this one,* his voice finished.

Amira heard the door open, and a quick rush of muffled conversation reached her. Events were stacking upon one another like children's building blocks, but she had no control over them. With no control, they'd collapse upon her and pin her beneath the weight, and she'd be left flailing against an immovable force. And when that happened, her life would end. Of that, she was certain.

The only consolation was that her longtime friend and fellow agency employee, Elizabeth Cathy – Beth to her friends – must have safely left their lunch at the Mezeh Mediterranean Grill. She'd been friends with Beth since her early days at the Farm, where the agency trained its new case officers, among others, in the National Clandestine Service.

Elizabeth had reached out to Amira a few months ago, having just returned from a tour as the Deputy Chief of Station in

Paris, a deceptively rigorous location from the constant threat of radical Islamic terrorism omnipresent in France. She'd heard about Amira's father and thought it would be beneficial if the two had lunch. For Amira, it was the first normal conversation she'd had with someone outside of Task Force Ares, and she'd embraced it, opening up to her friend as much as she could without compromising her position on the task force. After lunch, they'd enjoyed a delicious cup of coffee, and then she'd felt a little tired, chalking it up to the emotional release of sharing some of her grief with her friend.

Amira snapped back to the present. *The coffee. It was in the goddamned coffee. At least Beth got out,* although she thought it could be possible they'd kidnapped her, too. But if they had, they would've told her by now. Additionally, Beth would've been a loose end they didn't need. Amira was the real prize in the game whose clock had started.

All thoughts of Beth Cathy were wiped away from the surface of her mind at the appearance of the three new arrivals. *No. It can't be.*

This time, Samuel smiled broadly, the pleasure evident in the malicious grin. "I believe you know my good friend here, Trevor Emerson, a former employee of your agency."

Standing before Amira was a man in his late fifties, a full head of black hair showing flecks of gray. His features were non-descript, minus the deep blue intelligent eyes with heavy lines beneath them that seemed tinged with both genuine happiness and

11

sadness at the sight of her. He'd maintained his weight, and he looked trim and fit for a man his age. At five-foot-ten, his overall appearance allowed him to blend into almost any situation, which had served him well for thirty years as one of the agency's most-experienced case officers and foreign asset recruiters.

"Hello, Amira," Trevor said politely. "I have to say, it's been way too long, and I so wish this were under other circumstances. But this is the life we chose, and we can never run from our choices. You know that better than anyone."

A wave of fury, hot and white, threatened to overwhelm her. The man before her was the ultimate insider threat, a retired agency employee who'd somehow turned his back on the very nation he'd protected for decades.

Amira's father had been murdered at the behest of the former vice president, the highest-ranking traitor ever to exist inside the US government, even though the public hadn't learned of his treachery, for reasons the current president and Task Force Ares had agreed would be in the interest of national security. But the righteous anger still burned, and she'd run out of patience with men like Trevor. *Maintain your calm, for your sake.*

"I wish I could say the same for you," Amira replied curtly. "I'd heard you'd become disenchanted with the agency. But this? I never thought you'd turn traitor, not after all you'd done in service of the republic."

"Like I said, it's a life full of choices, and I made several small ones years ago," Trevor replied, shrugging his shoulders slightly with utter indifference. "They say the road to Hell is paved with good intentions, but I don't think that's quite the case. I think it's paved with baby steps, small movements forward so tiny you don't realize how dangerous they are until you're surrounded by the warmth and flames of eternal damnation."

Amira scoffed at the explanation. "You take up poetry in your retirement? You fancy yourself a modern version of Dante? Don't delude yourself. You're no different than the traitors who've come before you. You might have your reasons, but it won't end well for you, no matter what you think."

"Actually, I think I'm quite different. I *see things through,* and I never hesitate to act, as you well know from the first day we met." The initial pleasure he'd displayed at the sight of her was gone, replaced by the reptile and survivor within, the alter ego that no one ever saw.

Amira knew this to be true. She'd born witness to it, for Trevor Emerson was no normal agency employee. He was the man who'd recruited Amira into the CIA and a way of life she'd always known would end in only one way – ruinous violence.

"And what exactly do you plan to see through today?"

"Easy. The assassination of the current director of the CIA, your friend and boss, Sheldon Tooney."

Amira stared at him, hatred and fear mixing in one sickening combination. "You can't be serious. You know you'll never get away with this, right? Even you have to understand that."

"Oh. I do. And technically, *I* won't be assassinating anyone. *You* will. After what you've been through, the loss of your father, it won't be hard to convince the agency that you snapped and sought revenge against those you believed responsible."

"They'll never believe you. Trust me when I tell you this. You have no idea what you're starting here. If you did, you'd walk away, right now."

"My dear, ultimately, it's irrelevant. I just need the window of time that the confusion and your perceived involvement will cause. My friends and I will be out of the country by the time they untangle this web I've weaved, with you dangling in the center, trapped in death." His words were spoken with the confidence of a man who was convinced of his success, even before he'd achieved it.

The gravity of the situation threatened to pull her under. She shook her head in denial, and her chin fell to her chest as she tried to manipulate her wrists. *How had this come to pass, that the man who'd brought me into this business, a man I'd trusted with my life, a man whose life I'd saved, would be the one to end me?*

Part I – A New Way of Life

Chapter 1

The Clarice Smith Performing Arts Center
University Of Maryland School Of Theater, Dance, & Performance
Studies
Years Earlier
9:37 PM

Amira Cerone was exhausted, but like her father relentlessly
– albeit supportively, she had to admit – told her, "There are no
short cuts. You either put in the work, or you don't." As a testament
to her father's philosophy, her life as a junior at the University of
Maryland in the School of Theater, Dance, & Performance Studies
was about anything other than shortcuts. Between a double major
with a bachelor's degree in dance and another in criminal justice –
which made her father quite pleased – and the endless hours of
training and practice she put in at the Clarice Center, she barely had
time to breathe. Add the three times a week she trained in Chinese
kung fu in College Park just off campus, and it was no surprise that
her social life existed on a scale from zero to none. But she was fine
with that, as it suited her quiet and calm disposition.

There'd never been a doubt as to where she'd attend college,
and once she'd been informed that she'd been selected to receive a
Banner/Key Scholarship that paid for all tuition, room and board,
and additional expenses, the proverbial deal had been sealed. A full
scholarship to UMD's TDPS would've covered her full in-state

tuition, but as a resident of Washington DC because of her father's career as a police officer, she was considered out of state. But the Banner/Key had solved that financial dilemma in one fell swoop, and the school was thrilled to have her.

Then again, she'd known any school would've been, as she was the banner – pun intended, she always told herself – student: brilliant, hard-working, talented, and beautiful in form, physique, and function. The reality was that students like Amira Cerone were rare, and the school protected and coveted her like a sparkling treasure. Had it not been for her upbringing as the daughter of an Italian detective and Ethiopian immigrant – both whose work ethics rivaled Amira's – the attention TDSP heaped upon her might have gone to her twenty-year-old head. But she was not like other young women her age, and while she was grateful for the attention, she was also mature years beyond her current phase in life.

She breathed deeply, her body attuned to her surroundings, her legs in full contact with the stage as she sank deeply into the front splits. The Kay Theater was the school's premier classic theater for plays, dance performances, and ceremonies. Seating six hundred and twenty-six attendees, it currently had an occupancy of one – Amira. She loved the privilege of training alone on stage with only her focus and dedication to motivate and move her. The fact that the theater had a noiseless ventilation system only added to the experience. She was convinced that someday she'd perform on bigger stages – hopefully with a company like Bill T. Jones in NYC – and the sooner she was comfortable with all eyes on her in a setting like the Kay Theater, the better it would be for her career. She smiled to herself, engaged in an internal conversation. *You've been comfortable on these stages since you were nine and danced at the National Mall Christmas Tree lighting. True, but you can never practice too much. It's about the progress, not perfection.*

No TDSP classes were held after 5 PM for the purpose of providing the students the opportunity to rehearse and train in the evenings until 11 PM. Each student had a badge that provided electronic swipe access to the facility. The instructors urged the students to stick to the 11 PM cut-off time, but it wasn't a rarity to find a student or two somewhere in the facility at 2 AM. Youth, energy, and ambition were a potent cocktail for combating the normal need for sleep.

Shouts from outside the theater interrupted her near-meditative state. A dull thump followed, as if something had struck a wall in the main lobby. Her sense of calm was replaced with alarm, a sixth sense she was convinced she'd inherited from her father. *The only other person in here tonight is Susan, but she's in Gildenhorn across the lobby.*

The Clarice was constructed by an architect whose guiding principle had been to configure the facility as if several Tetris pieces had been haphazardly arranged during construction, with hallways, rooms, and exits jutting off the facility at all angles. The four front doors emptied into the multi-storied main lobby, the Grand Pavilion, which led up a lengthy three-tiered, wide staircase to the upper pavilion. Skylights and support beams lined the ceiling and created the airy, spacious central area of the Clarice with the four main theaters situated off the long, ascending space. The Kay Theater was the first one on the right and closest to the main entrance. The Gildenhorn, where Susan trained, was further up and to the left, the second theater on the other side. It was possible there were other students practicing deep in the maze of the facility, but it was a Friday night, and while the other members of TDSP might be dedicated, unlike Amira and Susan, they also chose to engage in the typical college experience, which included the local bars and Greek party lifestyle on the weekends.

Susan Li was Amira's closest friend and confidante at the University of Maryland. They'd become inseparable since Freshman year and shared an off-campus apartment. Susan's parents had immigrated to the US from China when she was five, and she barely remembered her homeland. Her father was some kind of engineer, and her mother a mathematician, the combination which explained Susan's "secondary degree" in bioengineering. Amira had no idea what that entailed, but like she'd told Susan, who breezed through classes with an endless supply of 4.0s and no effort, it didn't sound easy. Different upbringings and goals aside, they shared a passion for dance, and the fact that Susan was five-foot-four, lithe, and petite, while Amira was a lean, ripped five-foot-eight made the two quite the pair at first sight.

After a brief moment of silence, there was a second thud, followed by a short scream that cut-off abruptly.

19

Amira's internal alarm erupted into action, her only thought, *Something's wrong with Susan.* Her concern for her best friend outweighed her sense of personal security. She raised herself out of the splits, and like the graceful and powerful athlete that she was, she leapt off the stage, landed on the carpeted aisle below, and sprinted up the aisle, disappearing under the balcony seating. She ran as if floating up the inclined aisle towards the back of the theater and the orchestra-level exit.

Within seconds, she reached the set of double doors, paused, and tried to quiet her mind and control her breathing. The right rear door opened directly onto the grand pavilion, and if she emerged too quickly, she'd reveal her presence to whoever was outside. She didn't know what was happening, but she didn't want to make herself vulnerable without gathering more information. *The most informed decisions are always the best ones,* her father's voice reminded her. And then her mother's voice, Amara's Voice of Reason, as Amira called it: *Just be careful, honey. Be smart.*

The shouts grew louder, the voice of an angry male drowning out all others. *He's speaking Chinese. Is her dad here?*

Amira slowly pressed the bar across the right door and waited as the internal mechanism released, freeing the door. She pushed outward, slowly exposing a sliver of view to the scene outside.

Susan was being dragged against her will by two men towards the front doors, her ballet shoes providing little traction against the carpeted lobby. She leaned backwards, as if trying to brace herself, but the men were too strong and pulled her forwards.

Your time is now, Princess, her father's voice spoke insider her head, and her mind accepted the truth of it. Her father had reminded her at various times throughout her life that all people were tested at some point on their journeys through life. For some, it came early; for others, later. It was in those moments that life-altering decisions were made, for better or worse. Many survived and endured, while others failed and died. It was the way of life and would never change. Her father was convinced of it.

Be true. Always, her mind replied, and Amira leapt into action before the men could react. She pressed the door open and slipped through, accelerating as she moved. Her bare feet softened her footfalls as she covered the thirty feet to Susan's abductors. Like onstage, she floated across the floor, but instead of focusing on grace, she channeled all of her strength into pure power, mixed with anger and outrage at the two men who threatened her best friend.

Less than five feet away, the men halted, suddenly aware over the sounds of Susan's protestations of the movement behind them. The man holding Susan's left arm turned his head just in time to see the force of the young woman swarm down upon him.

Amira launched herself into the air, her right leg extended with her right foot angled at ninety degrees in the perfect flying sidekick position. The bottom of her foot struck the man in the small of his back, driving the breath from his lungs and violently propelling him forward as he reflexively released his grip on

Susan's arm. As Amira landed on her feet, the man crashed into a couch for waiting guests and flipped head over heels over the back.

Amira turned to the second man and ignored Susan's stunned look of surprise at her sudden appearance. "Let her go. *Now.*"

Susan's second abductor, a Chinese male in his thirties with brown eyes and longish hair, as if trying to blend in on a college campus, released Susan's right arm, stepped back, and smiled. He stood a few inches taller than Amira, and his body language exuded confidence, even in the face of the sudden attack that had temporarily incapacitated his partner.

He's dangerous. The smile says it all, Amira's father warned.

"I don't know who you are, but Ms. Li is coming with us. You're meddling in affairs that don't concern you. I applaud your effort to save your friend, and I'm going to give you one chance to walk away. I hope for your sake, you take it."

"He's right, Amira," Susan said, defeated acceptance and concern for her friend evident in her voice.

She's trying to protect you, not save herself. You need to do it for her. Amira smiled at her friend, and a sense of calm washed over her, similar to the way she felt in the seconds before she performed onstage. *Except this stage is a battlefield.* "No. He's not," Amira said defiantly, and sprang forward before either Susan or the man could respond.

She slid forward and feinted a strike to his face with her left hand. He recoiled, turned to his left as he slid backward, and brought his right arm inward as if to deflect the punch…exactly as Amira had hoped.

In addition to Kung Fu in college, she'd been training with her father to box since she was ten. As a female fighter, there was only so much power she could wield, but she made up for it with blinding speed that her father told her could've made her a professional fighter if dance hadn't been her passion.

Amira slipped to her right, lowered her center of gravity, and delivered four powerful blows to the man's left side. The punches doubled him over, but he still lifted his arm to ward off additional attacks. Amira seamless shifted tactics, grabbed his wrist with both hands, swept her left leg forward into his left foot, and pulled the arm straight back in a wristlock. The combination of momentum and control as he lost his balance and footing resulted in Amira pulling him to the ground while maintaining tension on his wrist.

From Susan's vantage point, one moment the man who'd been in charge and threatened her and her family was standing there, the next moment, Amira had him on the ground with such speed and violence Susan was stunned at her friend's aggression. *She's some kind of warrior. My God.*

Amira felt a surge of something primal, a sense of satisfaction at the knowledge she'd just physically bested two men who'd tried to abduct her friend, her roommate. She felt no fear, only the calm, now with the addition of a sense of purpose, as if she were made for this moment. She welcomed the feeling, powerful in its strength and resolve. *This is what it truly feels like to win. But now, you need to end it and get Susan out of here.*

Amira leaned over her captive, his arm locked-out under her control. "You didn't hear me the first time, but I think you hear me now." There was a menace to her voice, a tone not even Amira recognized. She felt as if some force controlled her actions, as if she were possessed by another being. She looked up at Susan as she torqued the man's wrist. He exhaled sharply in pain. "Where's your cell? Mine's in the theater. I left it on stage when I heard the commotion. We need to call 9-11 and get out of here."

Susan shook herself from her reverie at her friend's actions and shrugged the teal backpack off her shoulders and let it drop to the floor behind her. She turned, bent down, opened the small compartment in the front, and retrieved the Samsung flip phone her parents had purchased for her.

The man in Amira's grasp finally spoke, gritting his teeth in pain. "It's impressive, your skills, I mean that, but this is only going to end one way. Let me go, *now,* and I let you go. This is your last chance."

Amira considered for a moment, and then applied more pressure, ignoring his threat. "Susan, call the police. *Now.*"

As her friend dialed for help, Amira knew it'd be several minutes before the College Park Police Department arrived. Her father had warned her that like most police departments, there were only a handful of officers on duty during any given shift. If something happened to her, she'd be on her own initially.

24

Fortunately, her father had prepared her for an eventuality she'd hoped would never come. As with most things, her father had been right once again.

"My name is Susan Li, and there's been an attempted kidnapping at The Clarice Smith Center on campus. My friend and I are here, and two men just attacked us. Send help, now!" she implored the 9-11 operator.

Amira looked up at the main entrance, which consisted of a main set of glass double doors and an additional glass door on each side, and panic set in for the first time since the confrontation had commenced. Two more men were illuminated outside, moving towards the front doors. Both were Chinese, but unlike the two men inside, both held black pistols. Amira's sense of preservation catapulted her into action.

"We have to move! Two men with guns are coming!" She hoped the 9-11 operator heard her, but it was irrelevant. She knew they were on their own. She felt a flash of rage and looked down, only to see the man she'd subdued smiling at her. *Go to hell,* she thought, released his wrist, and struck him in the chin as hard as she could with a right across. The downward force of the punch snapped his head to the right, and he fell to the carpet.

Amira turned, grabbed Susan's hand, pulled her into motion, and fled back into the heart of the lobby.

The two friends reached the first tier of steps when the double set of doors crashed open behind them. Amira released Susan's hand and bounded up the first three steps when gunshots roared through the enormous space, reverberating off the angles and surfaces of the lobby. The shots struck the theater wall to their right, well over their heads, and Amira realized they were warning shots. *They can't kill us. They need Susan alive.*

Susan screamed in terror, and Amira risked a glimpse backwards. The two men had reached their fallen friends, weapons pointed in the direction of the fleeing girls. The man Amira had knocked to the ground was on his feet, even as the two newcomers moved past him.

"I told you…not to run. What happens next…is all on you," he said in between breaths as he rubbed the left side of his face.

Amira reached the top of the stairs first, with Susan a split-second behind her. "Follow me," Amira said, and ducked down a short corridor to the right just past the Kay Theater. *This is really bad, at least for you.* They obviously needed Susan alive, but Amira was expendable. In fact, she was now the only witness to the crime, and like her father always told her about witnesses after years of investigating homicides in DC, the bad guys didn't like to leave them alive.

Chapter 2

The Kogod Theater was a small, multi-purpose theater without permanent seating. Instead, due to its theatrical lighting, it often served as the location for small theatrical performances, workshops, receptions, and even seated dinners. What made the Kogod unique was that it was literally a giant sound-proof box lined with black curtains across each wall. As a result, the students had appropriately nicknamed it the Black Box, often shortened to just the Box. When the doors were closed and the lighting off, it created an environment of pure, pitch, blackness.

Amira loved the theater for that reason alone. She'd spent hours in the dark, tuning her senses to detect the most minute changes around her. Her logic was simple – if she could move fluidly in the dark, she'd be that much more proficient in the light. It was a principle one of her early karate instructors had utilized, blindfolding the students once every other week to test their situational awareness as the sensei tried to touch them without being detected. Amira was proud of the fact that he'd never succeeded once with her.

Inside the Box, Amira turned and pulled the black curtains over the door, eliminating the glow of the exit sign above the entrance. "That should disorient anyone who comes in behind us. They'll have to fight the curtains and the dark. Come on. Let's get out of here. We can use the sliding door."

In the rear corner of the Black Box was a corrugated, tracked door that slid upwards to reveal the entrance to the enormous prop area that spanned the length of the Kogod and the Cafritz Foundation Theater next door. Through the prop area, they could exit into the back wing on the east side of the facility, where multiple exit doors awaited.

"Are you okay? Do you have *any* idea what this is about?" Amira asked. "Talk while we move, as we only have seconds before one of these bastards comes in here."

"Look at you," Susan replied. "My own personal savior. I had no idea my roommate was such a badass."

"Hey, I'm the daughter of a DC cop. What did you expect? And I had to come to your rescue. You pay half the rent on the apartment," Amira quipped, attempting to lighten the severity of the situation.

The two girls had traversed two thirds of the space when more gunshots rang out from the lobby. They froze as a scream rose into the lobby, followed by one more shot that cut it off.

"That's not good. At all. Let's get out of here."

They reached the corrugated door, and Amira bent down, released the floor latch, and pulled up. She'd done this simple act countless times in the dark before. *What's one more time?* A wash of light emitted into the Black Box from the prop area, eerily illuminating the large space in a warm glow, the direct light slicing across their legs.

"It has to do with my parents. They told me I had to come with them, that my parents were in danger. I initially believed them, until they refused to let me call them, and that's when I knew something was wrong."

"Good instincts," Amira said as she pulled the door upwards and held it in place. "Whoever these guys are, they're not the good guys. Let's go. You first."

Susan slid under the door, stood up on the other side, and grabbed the bottom of the door. "Your turn."

Before Amira could respond, more shots rang out from the lobby, and the door to the theater opened. Two men, including the one she'd subdued with a wristlock, burst into the theater through the curtains. *So much for disorienting and delaying them.*

The man she'd struck instantly saw her and raised his pistol. Amira's mind raced, but there was only one option. "Drop it and run! NOW!" Amira shouted with such fierce command that Susan released her grip on the door.

As the door slammed to the floor, the man fired, the muzzle flash highlighting his face like a ghoul's mask on Halloween. The round struck the corrugated door, and sparks flashed from the impact, but Amira was already moving to her right, deeper into the darkness.

Trapped with two men who wanted to kill her and kidnap Susan, her twenty-year-old mind reached a conclusion that would've caused most people to crumble in the face of mortal peril – she had to incapacitate or kill them both, or she would die. She knew what her father would tell her to do, *demand* of her, given the situation. *I won't let you down, Daddy.*

Chapter 3

Get your breathing under control, or you're dead. She'd accepted her situation – kill or be killed – but she had no weapons, other than her bare hands. *You have to close the distance and disarm and incapacitate him, one way or another. Consider this on-the-job training. Beats a college internship.*

As calm as her outward movements were, the terror threatened to consume her. It was a suffocating, overwhelming sensation, the living embodiment of paralyzing nightmares in which she was stalked by a nameless, faceless being, a thing that moved with malevolent purpose. She fought the terror and moved to her right as her eyes and ears adjusted to the blackness.

Shoes scuffed the floor thirty or forty feet away. The exact distance was hard to pinpoint, since the Black Box was fifty-three-feet long and fifty-three-feet wide with a ceiling nearly thirty-feet tall. She placed one foot in front of the other and moved towards the sound. *The darkness is your weapon. Use it.* Her father, once again encouraging her to do the improbable, no matter how daunting.

Her heart pounded in her head, and she willed her heart to slow, although she wasn't sure it had an effect. More sounds of movement, from her right this time, and she realized that the two men had separated in *different* directions once they'd entered the theater. *Good. That makes your job easier.* She had a simple choice – right or left – and she chose left, only because she'd already started moving back in that direction.

A heavy breathing erupted from her right, twenty feet away, but she ignored it. As her father would've told her, neutralize the immediate threat first. He'd been in a shootout after a bank robbery in DC several years ago, when he and her mother had been engaged, and he'd shared with Amira when she was sixteen what it had been like, his story told in the form of a lesson.

Amazingly, the bank manager had triggered the silent arm and *not* been killed by the robbers, unaware he'd signaled for help. When they exited the bank, Nick Cerone and his partner were waiting for the perpetrators, guns drawn, standing behind the open doors of their police cruiser. The two robbers hadn't even hesitated – they'd opened fired with TEC-9 9mm automatic pistols with 30-round magazines, the street gangster's weapon of choice at the time. Both Nick and his partner, a big African American named Lesley Brown who'd grown up on the streets of DC, ducked behind their cruiser as the bullets peppered the vehicle. In that moment, Nick's fear had transformed into resolve, as he realized if they didn't take down the shooters, innocent bystanders would die, and for the two DC police officers sworn to serve and protect, that was unacceptable. They waited until the magazines emptied, and both Nick and Lesley stood, aimed, and fired, striking each robber multiple times, ending the gunfight. The two robbers had both bled out within a minute on the sidewalk, and neither Nick nor his partner mourned their loss. The lesson for Amira had been simple: *once you commit to a course of action that you know is right and true, you have to act, no matter what.*

Fully committed, she closed the distance and took several soft steps, moving in total silence. A half-muttered exclamation emanated from the dark no more than ten feet away. *He bumped into the rear wall,* which further honed Amira in on her target. She moved a few more feet and stopped as the man also froze, as if sensing her near him. *Don't. Make. A. Sound.*

She waited, the tension threatening to drown her once more, but the moment passed, and the man moved, only feet away from her. She heard his panicked breathing, and she realized he was directly in front of her, his arms likely facing to her left. *If you're wrong, you might get shot in the face, in which case, this will be over sooner than you know.* But she was out of time and out of room. *Now.*

Without the benefit of sight, she visualized the attack in her mind's eye and pictured the man, his arms extended forward, the pistol held chest high. Amira sprang forward and reached out with both her hands, literally grasping in the dark, praying she'd estimated correctly.

Her left hand crashed into a hard object, and she realized she'd struck the pistol. Her right hand struck something both hard and soft – *his face* – and she pushed as hard as she could, driving his head through the curtain and into the concrete wall. She was rewarded with a sickening smack as his skull collided with the concrete, but she didn't care. She grabbed the pistol with her left hand, wrapped her fingers around the top of the gun, and dug her right hand deep into his thick, black hair. Like her father had told her, *Unlike the movies, in reality, you make sure your enemy is down, no matter how many times you have to strike.* She yanked backwards and then slammed his head against the wall with as much strength as she could muster. He'd already begun to collapse from the first blow, which provided Amira with additional vertical downward force. His head struck a second time, and she was fairly certain she felt *and heard* a crack. *Good. He's out of this fight.* He crumpled to the floor and lay still.

She pried the pistol from his limp fingers, ducked down into a squat, and slowly moved to her right, the pistol straight and out, scanning for a target, the way her father had instructed. She had no idea what kind of gun she held, but she kept her finger straight and off the trigger. Her father was right, once again – the hours of training with him on the range had automatically switched on when she needed them. There was something to be said for muscle memory in the height of chaos and combat.

The second shooter whispered something in Chinese in an attempt to communicate with his partner. His only response was silence. *He now knows he's alone. You're only going to get one shot at this.*

Amira and the second gunman were locked in a Mexican standoff, and both knew it. She had to assume he knew she had his partner's weapon, and whoever fired first would reveal the other's position. She needed to create a diversion and force her enemy to act.

She reached down and grabbed the first thing she touched – the fallen man's shoe – and pried it off his foot. She cocked her arm back and threw it as far as she could towards the opposite corner of the Black Box. The shoe landed with a thud and tumbled two more times before coming to a rest.

There was a movement to her left and in front of her, but no shots came. *He's smart. He won't be tricked that easily. He also might know where you threw it from. Move.*

Amira's mind and body were in complete synchronicity, and she moved to the right as quickly and quietly as she could. She covered ten silent paces and stopped as she heard more movement as he crept towards where his partner lay against the wall.

More shots rang out from the lobby.

What's going on out there? The cops can't be here yet. It doesn't matter. Be patient, no matter what. Something will give. It always does, her father's voice said soothingly. *You've already evened the odds, and he may be scared because he knows he underestimated you. He'll make a mistake, and then he's yours.*

The fact that she welcomed the feeling, the anticipation of potentially vanquishing a second opponent who wished her harm, registered, but she pushed it aside, and waited.

Her terror had transformed into a fierce determination, that no matter what happened, she would not lose this fight, not to some *interloper* who'd assaulted her and Susan in the place they considered their second home, their sanctuary. It would not stand.

The entrance to the theater suddenly opened, and the lights from the corridor pierced the darkness, the amber glow freezing the scene inside the Black Box in the dull light. Multiple events occurred at once, and Amira acted without hesitation.

A man suddenly appeared in the doorway, crouched low as he moved, his silhouette shifting the shadows like living ghosts around the funnel of light inside the Black Box. Amira turned towards the light and spotted her adversary, the man she'd disarmed in the lobby. He stood thirty feet away from her, but his attention had turned towards the door. He raised his pistol, said something in Chinese, and waited for a response. Amira shifted the pistol towards her attacker, but time seemed to slow. She knew what was about to happen and prayed for another second to act.

The newcomer didn't reply, which sealed his fate.

He knows this new guy isn't one of his. He's going to shoot him. A coldness burst in Amira's chest at the knowledge that she had no choice, that she had to take a life to save a life. *The enemy of my enemy is my friend.*

Amira screamed, "Get down!" and fired, pulling the trigger smoothly several times.

The gunshots *roared* inside the confined space, the muzzle flashes bursting before her eyes with each squeeze of the trigger, but she held true and aimed at her target through each buck of the pistol. His body jerked as the bullets struck him in the side, left shoulder, and neck, moving in the dim light like a spastic ballerina. In his death throes, he managed to pull the trigger, but the man in the doorway had heeded Amira's warning and flung himself to the floor as she'd begun to pull the trigger. The Chinese attacker's final act in life, an attempt to kill another human being, ended in failure as his round went high and struck the door frame. He crumpled to floor of the Black Box and twitched as his lifeblood escaped and death consumed him.

Amira's adrenaline spiked, and a roar unleashed itself inside her head, mixed with a buzzing triggered from the deafening gunshots. Everything was muffled, but she breathed through it, knowing her hearing would return. The man she'd saved shouted at her, but she couldn't discern the words, drowned out by the sound of her heartbeat and the buzzing inside her head.

The man in the doorway moved into the Black Box, and he looked at her, his pistol aimed at the floor but in her direction, just in case she might be a threat.

A dam burst inside her head, and sound roared in with an intense split-second of vertigo, although the buzzing loudly remained.

"Ms. Cerone, I said, 'Are you hurt?' I'm with the FBI. Is there anyone else in here? And can you please lower that weapon?"

He knows my name. How? And then it hit her – *Susan. She made it out and somehow got help.*

The revolutions in her mind caught back up to the pace of reality, and she lowered the pistol, a flood of relief that the violent encounter had ended. *You did it, Princess. I knew you could.* The love she felt in that moment for her father enveloped her.

"There's another one behind you," Amira replied, pointing with her left hand, the pistol in her right. "I don't know if he's dead. I slammed his head against the wall pretty hard." She heard the crack of his skull in her own head and shook it off. "Who are you?"

"I'm with an FBI task force, but I'll explain later. First, is there a light switch in here? Also, the man you shot, you think you can kick that pistol away from him, if you're up to it? I need to secure this other guy in case he wakes up."

Up to it? Before she could catch herself, Amira shot back defiantly, "I shot him. I think I can take his gun, too."

The man paused at her confidence and fierceness, stared at her briefly, as if seeing her truly for the first time. He nodded, and said, "I'm Trevor Emerson. And I have no doubt you can."

Chapter 4

The aftermath of the combat – which is how Amira's mind catalogued it – felt like a Sunday drive of serenity compared to the chaos and violence of the encounter. She and Susan sat on the couch in the main lobby, the same one she'd kicked the first attacker over, as College Park Police, federal law enforcement, and paramedics swarmed over the scene in the lobby and the Kogod Theater. The final body count had not fallen in favor of Susan's abductors – three had been killed, and the one Amira had knocked unconscious had been airlifted to DC's MedStar Washington Hospital Center trauma unit. His skull was fractured, and the paramedics weren't sure he'd survive a lengthy ambulance ride.

Unbeknownst to Amira and Susan, once they'd fled into the Black Box, the gunshots they'd heard in the lobby had been Trevor Emerson and his FBI partner engage and neutralize – fatally – the two additional attackers they'd seen approach the entrance. Shattered glass and the two bodies, covered in white sheets, lay just inside the double set of doors.

FBI Special Agent Carter Johnson had immediately informed Susan that her parents, who lived in northern Virginia and worked in DC, were safe under the protection of a team of FBI agents.

"You know why they targeted me, don't you?" Susan asked Special Agent Johnson.

He was in his late-thirties, short brown hair, deep lines under his eyes for a man his age. He exchanged a look at Trevor, who shrugged and nodded, and responded, "I do. I think some of it should come from your parents, but what I'll tell you is that these men worked for the Chinese government, specifically, their intelligence service, and they were trying to use you as leverage against your parents. But I think the rest should come from them. You should know you and your parents aren't in any more danger. The US government is going to ensure that. In fact, your parents are very brave, honorable people, but like I said, you need to talk to them."

Susan nodded and pulled tighter across her shoulders the warm blanket the paramedics had offered. With the front doors propped open and shattered, the cool November air had invaded the space, creating a chill that touched everything in the lobby.

Amira squeezed her friend's hand. "At least this is over."

Susan looked at her friend, her eyes welling up. "I owe you my life. *Thank you,*" she said, her voice thick with emotion. She reached out and hugged Amira, forging a bond the two would never break. "Love you," Susan added with sincerity and no awkwardness.

"Love you, too," Amira replied.

"Ms. Cerone, can I speak to you separately?" Trevor asked.

The two girls disengaged, and Amira looked up at Trevor. "Sure. My parents won't be here for another fifteen minutes or so."

Amira had called her father as soon as she'd retrieved her dance bag from the Kay Theater. She'd conveyed to him the basic outline of what had happened, he'd told her how proud he was of her, that he loved her, and then he'd let her mother, Amara, talk to her, comforting her in a way that only a mother could. She'd tried to explain to her mother that she was fine, but her mother had insisted that they'd come and get her at the Clarice. While the FBI would be keeping a protective detail on Susan until her safety had been ensured, Amira had acquiesced to their demand to drive her back to the apartment when the police were finished taking their statements.

Trevor led Amira to the top of the steps in the back of the lobby, where the upper pavilion overlooked the enormous space. Trevor took a seat in a plush chair and motioned for Amira to do the same.

Trevor Emerson had a lean physique, a short beard, hair swept backwards and parted on the left side, a little longer than a banker or some other executive might wear it, and deep blue eyes that revealed an awareness and heightened level of intelligence. He was in his mid-forties, but he looked several years younger than his appearance.

Amira studied the man for a moment, who sat quietly watching her, and blurted out, "You don't work for the FBI, do you?"

Trevor smiled. "What makes you say that?"

"My father is a DC homicide detective. He told me that most of the FBI agents are clean-cut, by-the-book types in dark suits. You, with that beard, your hair, your *entire* demeanor, you

41

don't strike me as that kind of guy. You're something else, aren't you?"

Trevor's brow dipped for a barely perceptible moment. "I have to be honest. I'm trying to figure out what to make of you."

It was Amira's turn to raise her eyebrows, slightly offended, a tinge of anger filling her. "After what happened here tonight, that shouldn't be too hard." There was a steel to her voice that hadn't been there before, and she welcomed it.

Trevor suddenly leaned forward in the chair, his deep blue eyes fixing on her pale ones with intensity. "Let me ask you something – how do you *feel* about what you did? At twenty-years-old, you took a life, committed the ultimate act of depriving another human being the remainder of their existence. It's something you'll carry with you for the rest of your days." He paused to allow the gravity of the words to sink in. "Your skills exceed probably everyone your age and most of the people already in my line of work. I assume your father trained you, but it's more than that. My guess is that you're one of the driven, people who are called to excel at everything they do. I've seen it before, but I have to admit, usually it's cultivated, developed over time. But you, you somehow activated it on your own, and it saved your life tonight, at the expense of others. So I ask you again – how do you *feel?*"

Amira had been pondering that very question since her adrenaline had subsided. *How am I supposed to feel? I killed another person.* She thought society dictated that she felt some kind of guilt over it, over what the Catholic Church considered a mortal

42

sin. But she didn't feel guilty, not even the tiniest bit. In fact, she was proud of what she'd done. She'd protected and defended herself and Susan, and she'd beaten four men with bad intentions who likely would've killed her. *No guilt in that.* And then the word struck her, and she knew it was the right one.

"Triumphant. I *feel* triumphant. I did what I had to do, and I don't feel badly about it. Some might argue I should, but I don't. If I hadn't acted, Susan would've been kidnapped, and God knows what these men would've done to her and her parents. And once I confronted them, I knew they'd kill me. So I did what I had to do, and I'll never second-guess myself. Ever." The finality in her voice was filled with power and confidence.

She's a warrior, and she's just now realizing it, Trevor thought in awe at the beautiful, fierce, young woman before him. "What you feel, it's similar to what soldiers feel after combat, after they've vanquished an enemy trying to kill them. It's normal. It's what they trained for, and the fact that you somehow know it, without being in the military or law enforcement, that makes you special."

Amira nodded, accepting his praise quietly and with self-realization that what he spoke was true.

"And to answer your initial question, no. I'm not with the FBI," and he smiled, warmly grinning. "I'm with that other agency that people don't like to talk about."

"The one where they always say that stupid joke: 'I could tell you, but I'd have to kill you?'"

Trevor laughed. "Yes, but I can tell you, *and* we only kill people – like you did tonight – when it's necessary." The smile faded at the declaration of truth. It was a hard business he practiced, where transactions were often made in blood payments. "So here's the deal: you're a junior, and you have your senior year left after you make it through this one. I have no doubt you're an outstanding dancer, probably one of the prized students here. But what you just went through, I believe it changed you, and I think you know it. And if I'm right, I want to offer you a different way of life than the one you have planned. I don't want you to answer me now. I think it will become evident to you in the coming months. It's a hard life, and you'll have to make sacrifices. It can be dangerous, depending on which way you want that path to go, but in the end, there's nothing more rewarding than serving your country and protecting those who can't protect themselves, *just like you did here tonight.*"

The raw truth sent chills up and down her spine. *He's right, and you both know it.*

Trevor stood and reached inside his jacket. He pulled out a business card and handed it to her. His name and a cell phone number were the only things printed on it. "You enjoy the rest of your junior year. Take the summer, too. And next Fall, on your first day of your senior year, you call me, and we'll see what's what."

Amira accepted the card, and said, "Thank you," which had nothing to do with the card but the words and sentiments behind them.

Trevor nodded. "You earned it. Now, I'm going to leave you here to do something the rest of these people wouldn't understand."

"What's that?"

Trevor smiled. "Enjoy the moment and the glory," he said, and walked away.

Less than a year later, a call had been placed, and a new way of life had been offered and accepted, and Amira Cerone had never looked back.

Part II – Apex Predator

Chapter 5

Gaylord National Hotel
The Present
1545 EST

Assassinate Tooney? These people are crazy.

"And how pray tell do you plan to frame me for assassinating Director Tooney when he's over at Langley, and I'm tied up here? I'm pretty sure you don't have the technology to teleport."

Trevor laughed, smiled, and shook his head. "You really don't know, do you? I always find it astounding when the smartest, most talented people in the world – and you are one of those, Amira; I'll admit that – miss the obvious when it's right in front of their face."

Amira didn't respond, as she knew whatever came next, it wasn't going to be good.

"Didn't you notice all of the increased activity around the National Harbor? Large groups of people in suits, more than on any normal day of holiday shopping? Even the Harbor's own contracted security company has more patrols today than usual. Want to take a guess why?" The smile reappeared on Trevor's face, a mask of pure smugness.

What did I miss? She'd admittedly been so excited about her lunch with Beth that she hadn't considered the environment. It was the National Harbor, after all. Minus one poorly planned conceptual terrorist attack that the Prince George's County Police Department had foiled, it was a fairly low-threat environment. Amira remained silent in her refusal to placate her former mentor's ego.

"Fine. Since you won't play… Today, at the illustrious Gaylord National Resort and Convention Center, marks the beginning of the annual Intelligence and National Security Summit," Trevor declared. "And want to guess who one of the keynote guest speakers is for the final main discussion of the day, which starts in…" Trevor glanced at his watch. "…fourteen minutes, to be precise."

The annual summit was the premier forum for unclassified discussions between members of the Intelligence Community and other government agencies and their partners in both industry and academia. The topics ranged from evolving global threats to current trends, with a focus on developing collaborative solutions. It was a who's-who in the intelligence zoo and always garnered international attention.

The revelation hit like a physical blow, threatening to deflate what little hope she had. She should've known. Everything had been orchestrated to lure her into the trap that had been set, and she'd walked willingly into it. *But that means…* She'd dwell on that problem later.

"I know. It's brilliant, isn't it? And guess who has personal contacts with the private security company the Gaylord hired to protect this little soiree?"

"You're pretty pleased with yourself, aren't you?" Amira asked, even as her tactical mind reoriented itself to elicit more information on the soon-to-be-assassination attempt. "You thought of everything, didn't you? You always were good with planning. Let me guess: there's some look-alike of me running around downstairs in the convention center, likely with a back-up team in case something goes wrong?"

"See? I knew you'd figure it out. And like I always told you, the best plans are the simple ones. Less moving parts, the less that can go wrong."

The main door to the suite opened and closed, and she heard a male voice, thick with the same Dinka accent of her captors. *Jesus Christ, how many people are they bringing up here?*

"Just tell me one thing, Trevor – who's paying you to do this job?"

Trevor's smile vanished, replaced with an accusatory stare. "How many people have you killed, Amira? How many enemies have you made? I told you on the day we met that sacrifices get made in this business, but what I didn't understand back then – not really – is that to win in this business, you have to *sacrifice your soul.* And whether or not you realize it, you're well on on your way to paying that price. But I think you know that. Look what this job has taken from you. You lost your *father* because of this business."

Amira's fears were swept away at the mention of her beloved father, and all that remained was the fury and righteousness she carried into battle. "How *dare* you mention him to me," she said so quietly with such ferocity that all sound ceased inside the suite. "I don't know how, but you're going to die this day, and I pray I'm there to witness it."

Trevor nodded. "I know you believe that, and you probably have reason to, considering all you've done, but your time is running out. In fact, you have less than thirty minutes before you become another star on the agency's Memorial Wall. Goodbye, Amira. It's been an honor."

Trevor abruptly turned and left the room, abandoning Amira momentarily to her thoughts. *This can't be how it ends. I have to get out of this, somehow.* But she also knew that every other captured operative, soldier, and civilian thought the same thing, usually right before they died. As her hopes dwindled by the minute, no matter what, she'd hold on to them until her last breath. *It's who you are, until the end of your time,* her father whispered silently to her. *Don't give them anything else.*

The conversation in the living room ended, and Nafisa, Samuel, and the newcomer entered the bedroom.

Amira's mind froze for a split-second as she was once again greeted by an apparition from her past. *No. It can't be.*

"Hello, Amira. It's been a few years, although I didn't know your name back then," the South Sudanese man said. He was slightly shorter than Samuel, stockier and built like a body builder. His head was shaved, and he still wore a full beard similar to the day she'd first met him. "I'm just glad everyone in American shakes hands with their right hand; otherwise, it'd be kind of hard for me, thanks to you."

The man held up his hand, displaying for all what Amira already knew: the fourth and fifth fingers on his left hand were missing above the first joints past the knuckles.

I always knew leaving him alive was a bad decision. And now, it looks like I'm going to pay for it. God help me.

Chapter 6

Paloich, Southern Sudan
One Month Before the Events of OATH OF HONOR
0237 Local Time

Sudan had always been a country in turmoil. After nearly four decades of fighting, the rebellious southern region would hold its crucial referendum next month. The outcome was a foregone conclusion. There was little doubt to anyone paying even the most remote of attention that the people would vote for independence.

John Garang, the deceased leader of the Sudan People's Liberation Army, would finally achieve his goal, albeit from the grave. After all the fighting he'd caused, it had been a helicopter crash that had wiped him from the face of the earth, but his ultimate goal was at-hand.

Most in the international community knew better than to think that the South would declare its independence and stop fighting, not with everything at stake along the border. Treasured oil was buried in the territory over which they fought. No peace agreement could prevent further atrocities and bloodshed. It was naïve to believe otherwise.

Independence would be declared, but unimaginable human suffering had become a staple for the Sudanese people in those contested regions.

In addition to the war with the South, the government of Sudan had faced an uprising that started in 2003, when members of the Sudan Liberation Movement, supported by the Darfur Liberation Front, attacked the al-Fashir airfield in western Sudan. They'd destroyed four Hind attack gunships and killed most of the soldiers living on the base.

Khartoum's response had been swift and severe in the form of a ruthless genocide. They'd recruited the Janjaweed militias to exact revenge upon anyone unlucky enough to be associated with the rebels in any way.

Unfortunately, the meddlesome international media had leaked images of the horrors to the United Nations and other intrusive organizations. The UN indictments were jokes to Sudan's president and his advisors, reminders of the ineffective bureaucracy and hypocrisy institutionalized in luxurious office buildings in New York City. But then things had quieted down after the 2005 Comprehensive Peace Agreement with the South and the 2006 agreement with the Sudan Liberation Movement in Darfur.

But in the contested southern region, tensions continued for years, with attacks on the precious oil pipeline that ran from the Melut Basin – one of the richest sources of crude oil in Africa – more than fourteen hundred kilometers to Port Sudan. And at the very end of the pipeline lay the Paloich Pumping Station.

Operated by Petrodar Operating Company, a consortium of oil exploration and production companies, the pumping station was the sole source of activity in the impoverished Sudanese village of

Paloich. The facility was a sprawling complex more than six hundred meters long by more than three hundred meters wide. An endless array of buildings, production facilities, billeting, and enormous circular tanks were connected by metal tubes that moved the precious lifeblood of Africa along its evolutionary course. While multiple generators had been built inside the complex, the Paloich power plant lay adjacent to the facility and provided the power required to run the facility day and night. An impressive and ambitious operation, the problem was that the pumping station was self-sufficient, and the locals never received any of the financial benefits of having the pumping station located near their homes.

The native Sudanese locals lived in meager huts, eating peanuts with perch fished out of the contaminated White Nile fourteen miles to the west. Electricity was non-existent, as was school for most of the children. Since Petrodar had its own workers – mostly Chinese, Malaysians, Qataris, and Sudanese northerners – there were little job opportunities for the locals, and the consortium hired Paloich residents only for menial jobs. The bottom line was that Petrodar cared about the oil but not about the people. The only help came from an American aid group, which flew in food and medical supplies, as well as mosquito nets. It was this USAID-sponsored organization that provided the perfect cover for Amira Cerone, an operative for the CIA in their clandestine special access program known as LEGION.

USAID had flown Amira and several members of the US Embassy staff – including one doctor and one nurse – from

Khartoum via a C-17 to the Paloich Airport. They'd set up several tents, off-loaded the food and medical supplies, and spread the word to the local population that they'd remain for three days to treat the villagers.

For Amira, it was a break from the constant commotion and monotony of Khartoum, endlessly waiting for something to happen that might require the skills the CIA had spent millions on during her training. Not even the station chief knew her real identity or purpose. Only select senior executives at the highest level of the agency had access to LEGION and knew of its existence, which was why when the chat window on her ruggedized laptop popped open in the middle of the night, triggering a chime, she bolted upright from her cot.

She looked around the tent to ensure she was still alone and turned on a small portable lantern that filled the space with a dim glow. As the person in charge of the food supplies, she'd volunteered to sleep in one of the tents where the food had been stacked. She'd told her co-workers and the medical staff she'd be able to prevent any theft – which had plagued other humanitarian efforts – but the real reason was to afford her the privacy her real job required, as she was on-call for the agency twenty-four-seven.

She entered the password on her encrypted IBM Toughbook connected via cable to a small SATCOM antenna and generator just outside the tent. The chat window popped up, and she read the message. *South Sudan rebels attacked and captured the Paolich oil pumping station 5 miles to your southwest. Multiple casualties.*

55

Workers being held in the barracks. Estimated 10 enemy with small arms and automatic weapons. They've shut off the pipeline. Sudanese government coordinating a response, but they won't be able to reach the pumping station until tomorrow late in the day. Acknowledge.

Amira typed, *Acknowledged,* hit send, and waited.

We need you to infiltrate the pumping station, eliminate all hostiles except one, and get the oil turned back on.

Amira considered for a moment, and responded, *Why leave one alive?*

Because you need to send a message to the rebels that attacks like this are not in their best interest this close to the referendum. We're in negotiations with the GOS over a potential new oil field, and if you succeed, it will go a long way in achieving the US's larger objective. Please confirm.

Amira knew everything on the continent was about oil and other natural resources. *Mission confirmed. All objectives understood. I'll reach out once it's over. Out here.*

Good luck. God speed. Out.

Amira moved with purpose to a dark-green, footlocker-sized Pelican case with a spin-dial padlock. She entered the combination, lifted the lid, and smiled at the contents, pale-blue eyes glinting in the warm glow. *Tools of the trade. Time to get your game face on.*

Chapter 7

Paolich Oil Pumping Station
0403 Local Time

Asim Dafalla exited the operations center and stared upward into the African darkness overhead, the stars of heaven shining brightly upon him on the unusually clear November sky. The seventy-degree temperature felt cool on his dark skin, and he inhaled the humid air. *I should be resting. Omar would want me to. Tomorrow will be a long day.*

Omar Bol, Asim's best friend since the two were boys, was the leader the of the assault force that had captured the pumping station less than twelve hours ago. Unlike Asim, Omar was fierce and merciless, which explained why four of the security personnel at the station had been gunned down during the attack. Asim had quietly watched as one of the guards had tried to surrender, only to meet his fate from a barrage of AK-47 bullets from Omar. He'd felt sympathy for the guards, but he'd hidden his feelings, less Omar accuse of him of having mercy for the enemy. In Omar's view, the enemy was everyone associated with the pumping station, whether it be the workers, the owners, or even the few local Sudanese who were employed by Petrodar. They were thieves stealing the lifeblood of the earth, oil that should've been used to improve the living conditions of those who lived above it. *But that will all change, starting today,* Asim thought.

Omar had contacted Petrodar and informed them that the flow of oil was over. Their employees would remain hostages until southern Sudan was free from the iron fist of Khartoum.

When asked what demands he had, Omar had laughed. "Independence after the vote next month. Until then, your employees are *mine,*" and he'd disconnected the SATCOM phone call.

The plan was simple – hold the facility until the referendum was over and then demand improvements in the local infrastructure and living conditions for the residents of Paolich. And it was Asim's job to ensure that both their fighters and the hostages had enough food and supplies to last the next month. They knew about the USAID camp at the airport, and Asim planned to take four men with him to obtain the supplies, peacefully, he hoped.

He looked west across the facility, the structures jutting up into the night sky. It was eerily quiet, as they'd rounded up all the workers and placed them in a barracks adjacent to the operations center on the east side of the compound. Several of his fighters, believers in a free South Sudan, stood watch, while the other members of the assault force slept and patrolled the grounds of the facility in teams of two. Asim would figure out a permanent schedule tomorrow once the adrenaline from their victory had worn off.

He stretched his arms, his AK-47 slung over his shoulder. *Might as well take a walk and enjoy the silence while I can.*

Chapter 8

Amira studied the facility, patiently assessing the best infiltration point. The sprawling compound was a maze of buildings and pipes built around three enormous oil storage tanks – one next to the other in a row – that stood several stories and towered over the rest of the structures.

While there had been threats to the pumping station, the rebel assault had been the first actual attack. The isolation of the location had added a false sense of security, one the rebels had exploited on their first try. As a result, the facility had only been protected by a small cadre of armed guards whose effectiveness had obviously been insufficient for the task at hand, considering four of them were now dead. *Nothing like a homerun your first at bat in the Big Leagues of terrorism,* her father would've said.

She glanced at her watch. She had less than two hours before morning nautical twilight would begin, when the horizon would start to glow with the imminent sunrise thirty minutes later. But she planned to be long gone before the African light could reveal her presence.

She shrugged off her small, black tactical backpack and checked her weapons, securing the two fixed-blade, black stilettos and a suppressed SIGSAUER P229 9mm pistol in a holster that accommodated the suppressor. She adjusted her gear one last time and moved towards the northwest corner of the facility. She'd selected the remote corner as her infiltration point since it was the furthest part of the compound from the operations center and the barracks.

Her first objective was simple – enter the compound, move as quietly as possible under the cover of darkness, and eliminate all patrols. Considering the size of the estimated enemy force, she figured there were no more than a handful of men on duty. Once she cleared the exterior, she'd tackle the larger problem of freeing the hostages. *One thing at a time.*

Dressed in a skin-tight, black, long-sleeve compression shirt, black tactical pants, black Oakley hiking shoes, and a black neoprene balaclava that covered her head, her figure was nothing more than a lean, muscular shadow that moved through the darkness.

She reached her infiltration point and kept moving, the absence of a perimeter wall another tactical advantage. The maze of pipelines stretched out towards the east side of the compound, several hundred meters away. Using the pipes as additional concealment, she quickly and quietly crept towards the middle of the facility. The enormous tanks lay to her right, blocking out the sky. *Just keep moving. There have to be men out here somewhere. Not even a rag-tag bunch of rebels would leave the compound completely unguarded at night.*

Thirty seconds and another one hundred meters later, and two voices engaged in conversation reached her neoprene-covered ears. Amira froze and waited, her ears automatically zeroing in on the two men. Their voices grew slightly quieter, and Amira moved towards the space between the first and second storage tanks. *They're just around the curve, moving away. You'll catch them from behind.*

Shrouded in darkness since the architects had failed to have the foresight to install lighting at the base of the tanks, she crossed the open space between the pipes and the tanks. The sound of her footfalls barely reached her own ears, which reassured her that the two men would never detect her approach.

The voices grew louder, and she realized the two men had stopped moving, just out of sight. *What now?* Her internal inquiry was answered with the flick of a lighter. *Perfect. They're holding their cigarettes and not their weapons. Go now.*

A black stiletto in each hand, fingers wrapped around each grip with each blade pointing down, Amira stalked her prey, her feet moving swiftly across the dirt. She rounded the wall of the tank, the two men finally coming into repose fixed to the ground less than ten feet away. A force of nature that had been trained as one of the CIA's most lethal assassins, she struck the two rebels in a blinding flash of dark speed and fury.

Her final steps as she reached them alerted the two men, but by then, it was too late. Attacking from the left side of the rebel closest to her, she plunged the left stiletto into the side of the man's neck, lowered her center of gravity, and spun completely around to her right across the front of the mortally wounded man. She exited her spin directly in front of the second guard, who only had time to drop his cigarette, and plunged the right-hand stiletto into his chest just below his breastbone, piercing his heart. Both men collapsed to the ground, unconscious in their final death throes.

Their bodies stopped twitching, and Amira crouched motionless, waiting for the sounds of reinforcement. A minute ticked by, and then another. *Good. No alarms. Two down. Keep moving.*

On the south side of the huge tanks that towered above her, she moved east towards the single-story operations center, intent on her objective.

A low growl that grew in length and rose in pitch – ending in a solid note that reminded her of a whale and not a land predator – rose from outside the facility. Amira ceased her motion. A second growl-yelp joined the first. *Wonderful. Hyenas.* The aggressive animals were notorious night-time hunters. In a pack, they were apex predators, powerful killers, and mortal enemies of lions. A single adult spotted hyena could individually take down a wildebeest, even though the social animals preferred strength in numbers. A third growl-yelp joined the first two. *Definitely a pack.*

The three animals went silent, but Amira remained motionless. Thirty seconds later, the night calls started again, still south of the facility but closer to the perimeter near the east side. *They're hunting something.* And then it hit her, and Amira broke from her location, stretching her legs into a run.

She'd planned to create a diversion, but the Wild Kingdom event unfolding before her was better than anything she'd thought of to this point. Trevor Emerson's voice in her head approvingly said, *The greatest skill as an operator is to use the unknown to your advantage. If you can harness unforeseen events to suit your purpose, your enemy will never have a chance.* She thought he'd be especially pleased with what Mother Nature had thrown in her path.

Amira covered the open ground south of the tanks and reached the eastern man-made barrier of pipes that ran from north to south. Smaller buildings connected to the pipes up and down the line. Past the barrier, erected floodlights illuminated the operations center and the barracks building just south of it.

More growls erupted to her right, only a few hundred meters away and close enough to raise the hairs on the back of her neck and arms. *Christ. How many are there?* She discerned at least five, but their cries increased in intensity, mixing as their animal instincts escalated into a heightened sense of carnal thirst. *Their prey is close.*

Amira sheathed her two stilettos and unholstered the suppressed SIGSAUER P229. *Not going up against large killer canines with knives. Do or die. Time to move,* she thought, and ran from beneath the cover of the pipelines.

Chapter 9

Asim stood outside the door to the operations center, a long rectangular building that ran south to north. He'd returned from his walk at the sound of the first carnal cry. The hyenas had alerted the patrolling guards, and four of his men gathered in a group thirty meters in front of him, moving along the side of the barracks building where the hostages slept.

Asim knew the African animals were dangerous, especially at night. When he'd been a boy, a pack had infiltrated his village and killed two children who'd decided to sleep outside their hut. After the attack, the adults had established guards, and two nights later, they'd managed to kill two of the animals with machetes and AK-47s. He'd wondered at the time why the men had Russian assault rifles in a remote African village, but now, as an adult, he knew why: violence and conflict were the ways of Africa. *And until something changes, they always will be.*

The pack suddenly grew quiet, and the four armed men stopped moving, having reached the far end of the barracks. A row of trees had been planted just beyond the billeting in an attempt to provide a respite of outdoor shade to the workers who lived inside. Unfortunately for Asim and his men, the trees concealed the roaming pack of predators on the hunt.

The African night stood still, as if waiting for an invisible force to give the command to commence what Asim knew was coming. With the rebel attacks he'd led with Omar, it was always the quiet before the slaughter that was the most unnerving for him. The fact that a pack of hyenas had selected his men as prey only made it more chilling.

A single low growl emanated from just beyond the trees. *It's the female. She's giving the command to attack.* Asim knew the matriarch of the clan was the largest and most dangerous predator in the group, and he strengthened his grip on his AK-47.

Two sleek forms thirty feet apart exploded from the tree line, powerful legs and feet moving towards the men. Like bullets of animal fury, they covered the distance to the men in less than two seconds.

The man on the far left of the group managed to pull the trigger of his AK-47, but the bullets kicked up puffs of dirt as the first of the three-foot tall animals barreled into his chest, knocking him to the ground. The large animal dug its powerful jaws and head into his stomach, tearing at the soft flesh in an attempt to disembowel him.

The second man from the left froze in terror at the swiftness of the attack on his friend, and the second hyena leapt at him, even as two more hyenas emerged from the tree line, their rough paws propelling them across the dirt. The second monstrous beast tore into the man's upper leg, snarling and growling as it bit deeper into the flesh, blood pouring over its bristly muzzle.

Asim watched in horror as his remaining two men fired their weapons at the new shapes from the tree line. At least one of the beasts was hit, and its forward momentum was violently halted, tumbling end over end into the ground. The fourth hyena struck the man on the far right, sinking its teeth into the wrist of his trigger hand. The jaws crushed close, pulverizing the man's wrist into tiny pieces of bone and eliciting a shriek of horror from the rebel.

The remaining man on his feet turned to assist his friend, which exposed his back to the second hyena that had attacked and ripped apart the upper leg of the second rebel. The first two of his friends had already lapsed into unconsciousness from the sudden blood loss and shock. Death would follow soon.

The second hyena crashed into his back as he pulled the trigger on the AK-47, which caused the rifle of the weapon to lift, and bullets strafed across the back of his friend that he'd intended to help. The hyena scrambled up his back as the rebel's chest hit the dirt, and he felt powerful jaws clamp down on the back of his neck. He heard a crunch as the terror overwhelmed him, and then he felt nothing as the wild animal crushed his spinal cord.

Asim's mind fought to process the swiftness with which four of his men had just been literally torn to shreds. From beyond the three hyenas that continued to bite and tear into his friends, Asim saw two more shapes emerge from the trees. One was significantly taller than the other, with a larger and broader head. *God have mercy. The matriarch.* She stood at least four-feet tall and made the other hyenas in her pack seem like playful puppies compared to the menace that oozed from her muscular form. He raised his weapon to fire at the pack leader when a blur of black shadow appeared from his right.

His AK-47 still aimed at the hyenas, he turned his head and saw a figure clad in all black sprint across the dirt between him and the hyenas, moving rapidly towards the barracks building. *That's not one of ours.* And then his male mind registered the way *she* moved, the lean physique, the gracefulness. *It's a woman,* was his last thought as she extended her right arm towards him and opened fire with the pistol he hadn't spotted until she'd pointed it in his direction.

Fortunately for Asim, the suppressed shots struck the corrugated steel of the operations center behind him, and he ducked and turned in retreat. He moved towards the short stairs that led to the door to the center. *I have to warn Omar. We're under attack.*

Chapter 10

Assaulting an enemy position with a pack of hyenas as a diversion hadn't been covered at the Farm during her tactical training, but Amira didn't care. Her only concern was for the hostages in the barracks ahead of her.

Her approach had been shrouded in darkness, and since the rebels' attention had been fixed on the tree line and the snarling threat hidden beyond, she knew they'd never detect her until it was too late. The only variable had been the sole rebel near the entrance to the command center, but once the bloody hyena attack had started, he'd been transfixed on the horrifying fate of his men. It was the perfect moment amidst her own fear of the wild animals to commence her own assault.

Now, as she sprinted for the barracks building, she maintained a path at least thirty feet away from the four men who lay dying as they were devoured alive. The only one still screaming was the man who'd had his wrist crushed into tiny fragments, but his suffering would be short-lived as another hyena left its fresh kill to help its packmate finish him.

As she ran, she spotted the large female and smaller male nonchalantly move towards the hyena kill zone. *She's big and no doubt she's mean. Steer clear.* While she considered herself an apex predator in the jungle of her career field, Amira had no intention of tangling with the matriarch.

With her SIGSAUER held to her chest, her right elbow bent as she ran, she turned back to the sole rebel still alive and discovered he'd finally spotted her, fifty feet from the barracks and the door on its end. *Six dead hostiles. Let's make him number seven.*

Without breaking her stride since she wanted to get past the hyenas as quickly as possible, she fired several shots in his direction. She knew they'd missed when he crouched down and fled towards the steps that led to the command center. *No worries. I'll deal with you later.*

With the sounds of tearing flesh and snarling, ravenous hyenas behind her, she ran hard, eager to not be their next meal. She reached the northeast corner of the barracks, a single-story building with a door that opened directly at ground level. She glanced back at the command center but no longer had a line of sight to the entrance, as the command center was slightly offset to the left of the barracks.

She crept forward, her pistol held in her right hand, her back near the wall but not touching it to avoid additional noise. The door lay less than ten feet in front of her. She wasn't sure what the layout inside was, but she knew one thing which gave her the confidence required – she was a *fast* and lethal shot, especially when engaging multiple targets.

The door flung outward, slammed into the wall less than three feet in front of her face, and bounced off, providing a small area of cover. Amira hid behind the door and waited. A rebel holding an AK-47 burst from the entrance, his assault rifle scanning the area for targets. He took two steps forward and stopped, and a second man emerged just behind him but froze instantly. Both men's gazes were fixed on the opposite corner of the building. *What is it?*

A low growl answered the question for her, which was the only cue she needed. She stepped out from behind the door, aimed her pistol at the back of the first man's head, fired, transitioned to the second man – who'd begun to turn – and fired again. In less than a second, both men lay dead on the ground, but Amira ignored them and kept her eyes on the enormous female hyena that moved out of the shadows and into the cone of the flood light mounted over the door. *She circled around the building. Clever beast.*

The beast was less than fifteen feet away from Amira, and her eyes glinted in the light like dark gems, staring at Amira. For the first time, Amira felt fear creep into her stomach. Her pistol was in the ready position, aimed at the dirt. She knew she had enough time to raise the barrel, fire, and hit the creature, but if she could avoid it, she would. She maintained eye contact and stood her ground.

The monster chuffed, and spittle flew from her wide head. The beast took a single cautious step forward, assessing Amira. The stench of blood rose into the air between them. Amira moved to her left, slowly, but kept the pistol pointed in the direction of the matriarch in case she had to make a quick adjustment. *A game of chicken with an African hyena. My dad won't believe this one…if you survive to tell him.*

The monster took a second step forward, and Amira followed with another step to the left. The hyena continued to stare at her and moved its head up and down, as if in consultation with itself as to the threat Amira posed.

Amira wondered if it knew that she was also a predator like the matriarch, a hunter of men. *Can she sense that? If so, maybe she'll respect it.* She stayed calm and waited for the hyena to make a decision. She realized she'd been so focused on the beast in front of her that she'd forgotten about the hostages inside. Voices and shouts leaked out through the doorway.

As if sensing her thoughts, the hyena took another step forward. Amira shuffled left one more time, but before she could react, the hyena aggressively bounded forwards…but not towards her.

In three strides, the monster hyena disappeared through the doorway, leaving Amira to fend for herself outside. *Oh no. The hostages.*

One of the original hyenas appeared from around the corner to Amira's right, blood thick and dark on its muzzle. In his case, Amira never hesitated. She raised the pistol and fired three rapid shots that struck the predator in the head and neck, its yelps of pain a chilling reminder that she was taking the life of an animal whose only crime had been to act the way its nature dictated. The animal fell to the dirt, dead.

She ejected the magazine, grabbed a spare from a pouch on her black web belt, inserted the near-empty magazine in its place, and slammed the fresh one into the well of the pistol. She pulled the locked-back slide just enough to release it forward and chamber a fresh round.

Screams reached her ears and were followed immediately by gunfire. *I can't believe I'm about to do this.* She moved through the doorway, the pistol up and ready to engage.

Chapter 11

The inside of the barracks was a scene of dimly-lit chaos and carnage. Someone had flipped a switch, but only two overhead lights illuminated the fifty-foot-long space. Several cots had been pushed up against the left side of the building, and a scattering of small tables and chairs marked the space on the right. Furniture aside, terror at the sight of the massive hyena had seized control of the scene, and her mind processed it all in a snapshot.

One rebel lay just to the left of the door, his AK-47 in his lifeless arms as blood poured from his shredded neck. After her first kill, the hyena had turned her attention to two rebels on the left, who tried in their panic to bring their weapons up. *She's going for the ones with weapons first. Somehow, she knows they pose the most danger to her. Smart girl.* Their line of sight had been blocked as the hostages scattered across the space in a mad dash towards the back of the building and a lone rebel who seemed frozen to the floor in fear. Two more rebels stood at one of the tables, AK-47s tracking the sprinting hyena. *Two on the right. Clear line of sight.*

She fired the SIGSAUER twice with perfect accuracy, and both men fell, one striking the table and flipping it, while the other tumbled over a chair. Between her and the hyenas, eleven rebels were dead. *Three more to go in here, and then you need to find the stragglers, including the one you chased back into the command center.* Amidst the chaos, no one seemed to pay attention to the black-clad killer among their ranks.

The hyena weaved in and out of the fleeing hostages as full-fledged panic spread across the room faster than a California wildfire. Amira moved towards the area of cots, combat-walking in an attempt to line up a clear shot on the two gunmen on that side of the room. No matter what happened, no hostage would die from a bullet fired by her.

The man on the right opened fired with his AK-47, the 7.62mm shots deafening in the enclosed space. Amira heard a cry of pain slightly in front of her and to the left as a hostage, hit by the bullets, fell forward mid-stride. *They're going to kill everyone. You need to stop them.*

She halted her movement, placed the sights on the chest of the man who'd fired the AK-47 but held fire as the last hostage from the left side of the room dashed across her view towards the back of the building. The moment he cleared her line of sight, she pulled the trigger smoothly, and her suppressed pistol added its sound to the cacophony inside. The rounds struck him in the chest, and his AK-47 grew silent as he crumpled sideways.

Operating solely by reflex, his partner, recognizing the new threat Amira posed, made the mistake of abandoning his original target. His slow attempt at drawing a bead on her gave the matriarch the precious milliseconds she needed to cover the remaining distance to him. The barrel of the AK-47 he wielded never came close as the hyena slammed into his side and lifted him off his feet like a professional linebacker tackling a pee-wee league player. The ferocity of the attack left Amira awestruck at the pure power of the hyena, but she focused her attention on the last rebel in the back of the room, who'd barely moved since the attack began. *He's in shock, which is good for me.* There were too many panicked bodies between her and him for a clean shot.

As terrorized men fled the unfolding death, Amira crouched and jogged forwards, keeping the throng between her and the last rebel. She glanced left and saw the matriarch with her nuzzle buried in her prey's chest, turning it into a dark, gory mess.

As if sensing her gaze, the pack leader looked up and fixed her intelligent eyes on Amira's, which sent a chill down her back. Amira reflexively nodded at the beast as if she could primitively communicate with her, and the apex predator dropped her muzzle back into the body of its warm kill.

Within seconds, Amira had closed the distance to the back of the room.

Less than fifteen feet away, the last rebel roused himself from his stupor. His eyes picked up her movement at the last second, and he realized with dawning horror that there were *two* threats inside the barracks, but only one was moving towards him. He slowly raised the AK-47 in her direction, when an arm appeared from behind him. It snaked its away across his throat, as a second man stepped forward and plunged a large knife into the rebel's side. He shrieked in pain and instinctively dropped the assault rifle as the blade was forced repeatedly into his side, his back arching with each pierce of the steel. Moments later, his struggling ceased, and the man behind him released his hold, allowing the dead rebel to drop to the floor.

As if in unison, dozens of faces turned towards Amira. "I'm here to rescue you, although to be honest, the hyenas did more of the work than I had to," she said loudly and clearly. "Is there anyone here that speaks English and can translate to the others?"

Several men looked at each other, and an older Chinese worker in his late forties stepped forward. "I understand," he said in near-perfect English.

"Good," Amira replied, cutting him off. "First, do you have any idea how many more rebels there might be? I killed two near the tanks, two just outside of the door here, the hyenas killed four more, and then we have the six down in here. I chased one back into the command center."

"I believe there are two more," the man replied. "The leader, who calls himself Omar, and his lieutenant."

"Okay. In that case, I need you to gather the weapons from these rebels and stay in here until it's safe. I'm going to go take care of the last two and end this."

There was a shuffling behind her, and several men gasped in horror.

Even though she knew, she turned and faced the matriarch, who stood less than ten feet away, her muzzle dripping blood in large dark droplets. But even more alarming was the fact that two of the smaller males had silently entered the barracks and stood behind her on each side like royal guards protecting their queen.

Chapter 12

Omar stood in front of a large control panel which occupied the entire back wall. Computer monitors, keyboards, communication equipment, and workstations sat empty, their operators in the barracks building next door. The number of machines it took to run a facility like the pumping station was a mystery to Asim, who cared more about life's necessities such as food, water, clothing, and weapons than he did about technology. It had been a source of bemusement to Omar, who understood that the rebels had to embrace technology, if only to use it against its creators.

"What's going on out there?" Omar asked, concern in his voice. His loose clothing hung around his stocky frame, but he held his AK-47, ready for the fight.

"We're under attack. I only saw one of them. But worse, a pack of hyenas attacked at the same time. All of our men outside are dead. The intruder I saw ran into the barracks next door. Brother, we need to *leave* immediately. There have to be more of them, and after our losses, we don't have a chance. If we leave now, we live to fight another day. There is no good outcome if we stay. South Sudan will be ours soon enough."

Asim watched as Omar internally processed the information and struggled with himself as to how to respond to the attack. Asim knew Omar would welcome death if it served a higher purpose, but Asim was certain there was no purpose to be served by remaining.

"Okay. Let's get to the jeep," Omar said finally, and grabbed a set of keys from a rack that had been nailed to the wall next to the door.

The two men exited the command center, and the sounds of combat reached them from the barracks. Asim reflexively cringed at the two hyenas that continued to consume the corpses of his men. *God look over them,* he thought, and turned away. There was nothing left for him at this accursed pumping station.

Chapter 13

Amira sensed the fear of the men behind her, and she heard movement. *They've grabbed the AKs.* "No one open fire. Anyone who does, I'll shoot him myself," she declared clearly and loudly enough for the entire assembled mass of former hostages to hear. She didn't want to kill the matriarch or her male protectors unless she had no choice. The female hyena and her pack had been a force multiplier unlike any other, and she respected the beasts for what they were – like she was – *predators and hunters of men.*

She felt her heart pound in her chest as her adrenaline surge continued. The matriarch lowered its head, its eyes up and locked on Amira's face.

If that's what you want, fine. Amira slowly lowered the pistol and let her arm hang at her side, although she was confident in her speed to reacquire her target if the need arose. She carefully lifted her left hand, her eyes never leaving the matriarch's. She slowly raised the neoprene mask and rolled it up on top of her head, the back still tucked in below her collar. The men had shrunk back behind her, and she was certain no one could see her face in the gloom. *Here I am. See what I am,* she thought calmly, certain this was the right course of action.

The matriarch raised her head, her bright eyes studying Amira's face. Her nostrils flared, as if inhaling the scent of the person in front of her.

Amira felt no fear, and as the seconds ticked by, her confidence grew. *I'm just as much of a killer as you are. Understand and believe that.* She concentrated, as if willing her thoughts towards the matriarch. Amira was suddenly aware of herself, the blood on her clothes from the men she'd killed outside, the sweat and dirt on her face. *And she senses it, too. She knows what you are.*

The matriarch suddenly raised her head and let loose a cry, and the men behind Amira gasped in fear. The pack leader suddenly turned, barked its unique growl-yelp, and the two males who'd accompanied her turned and bounded for the door. The matriarch turned her head back to Amira one last time and launched herself towards the entrance. She loped across the floor, fast and sleek, and disappeared into the night.

A sense of pride and satisfaction coursed through Amira. The matriarch had encountered a fearsome hunter equal to herself, and she'd respected the law of the jungle. *I know what I am, and so does she.*

She rolled the neoprene mask back down over her face and turned around. The men stared at her in awe, not as the woman and killer before her but as if she were some kind of ancient goddess in human form.

Before she could speak to break their reverie, the faint roar of an engine entered through the open door. *Out of time.*

"Listen, help will be on the way. I'll make sure of it. Is there a vehicle around here? And where are the keys? I can't let these bastards get away."

The Chinese leader said, "There are keys in the command center on a rack right inside the door. There are three jeeps on the other side of the building. The top rows of keys are for those. Good luck," he said, and then added, "and thank you. We are in your debt."

"You're welcome. I'm sorry about your losses," she said, referring to the guards murdered during the initial assault and the additional hostage who lay dead on the floor, killed by the rebel's gunfire as the matriarch had attacked. "It's been interesting. Feel free to leave out the details of my arrival, if you don't mind. Take the credit. You all earned it. Be safe."

And just as quickly as the matriarch had fled the building, Amira sprinted to the door and exited as the stunned liberated hostages watched their rescuer pursue their remaining captors.

Chapter 14

Amira grabbed the last set of keys from the top row and dashed out of the command center, leapt down the short set of steps, and sprinted north. As she rounded the corner, she glanced down at the keychain and saw the Toyota symbol on the key, whose base was a remote FOB with lock and unlock symbols. She skidded to a halt, pressed the unlock button, and a second later, a chirp and the flash of headlights drew her attention to a white Toyota Hilux 4x4 pick-up, one of the most popular off-road vehicles on the continent. *We're in business.*

She reached the truck, entered the double cab, inserted the key, and slammed the center console gearshift into drive. She pressed the accelerator to the floor, and the vehicle lurched forward in the dirt, following the dust that still hung in the air from the fleeing rebels. *They're less than sixty seconds ahead of you. You can catch them.*

The network of pipes raced by on her left as she sped through the compound, the lingering dust in her headlights a suspended trail of breadcrumbs. She reached the end of the dirt road and slammed on the brakes. To her left was the northern perimeter of the facility – *don't forget to come back and get your backpack* – and to the right was the exit and the sprawling village of Paloich. She looked through the passenger window and was rewarded by a pair of headlight beams bouncing away into the night no more than a quarter of a mile from her location. *Gotcha.*

Amira turned off the main headlights, left the running lights on, and floored the accelerator. The Hilux roared to life and chased after the escaping vehicle. She hoped they wouldn't see her until it was too late, but no matter what, only one of them would survive the night. Her orders had been clear, and she planned to stick to them.

As the Hilux raced across the flat ground of the dirt road, she kept her eyes on the target vehicle. It had turned north away from her. She kept her eyes on the road and realized in the glow of the running lights that it gradually curved to the left. She accelerated through the gradual curve and hit a straight-away just as the vehicle in front of her turned right. *It's now on the paved part of the main road that runs through the area.* The Hilux picked up speed, and she glanced at the speedometer, which read 140 kph. *Damn metric system,* she thought, recognizing she was driving 85 to 90 mph.

The pick-up reached the turn less than twenty seconds later, and Amira slowed just enough to drift through it. The Toyota's tires gripped the pavement, and the Hilux shot across the road on its newfound traction.

Where the hell are they going? The main road turned left less than two miles away and ran north to the airport. Going straight, the pavement transformed into another dirt road. There were no other vehicles in sight, and Amira kept her eyes on the red taillights, which grew closer by the second.

The vehicle – another white Toyota Hilux, she was close enough to recognize – slowed down, its taillights blazing brightly in the morning darkness. Amira followed suit but kept gaining ground.

83

The second Hilux continued to decelerate, and Amira was forced to slow even more. She was less than thirty yards away when the Hilux ground to a complete halt, and Amira did the same.

For the briefest of moments, she wondered what their plan was, realizing an instant later their intent. *Ambush.*

Amira floored the accelerator as both the driver and passenger front doors opened, and a man appeared on each side, holding an AK-47 and turning it in her direction. Her Hilux shot forward as automatic weapons fired once again cried into the night.

Twenty yards, she thought, crouching low behind the steering wheel as the first rounds struck the hood of the vehicle. She pulled the steering wheel to the left at ten yards from the back of the vehicle and took aim at the driver.

Bullets ripped into the windshield, and one struck the mirror. Glass exploded around her, but she maintained her grip on the steering wheel. *Almost there.*

The man on the driver's side realized the danger too late. He turned, took two steps, and jumped into the air to reach the safety of the hood of the Hilux. The only thing he succeeded in doing was making himself a bigger target.

The grill of Amira's Hilux struck him flush on the right hip as he rose into the air. His body was violently spun as his lower body absorbed the impact. He flew across the hood of his Hilux and sailed several feet before landing on the pavement.

Even as his body hit the ground, Amira had slammed on her brakes. Her Hilux skidded to a halt as she fired the SIGSAUER through the passenger window at the second shooter, which forced him to take cover behind the passenger side of his own vehicle.

Amira opened the door and bailed out quickly, moving to the back of the vehicle. She wasn't sure if the man she'd struck had survived, which meant she had to take the remaining rebel alive, as she'd been instructed.

This job just gets harder and harder, which was why she'd brought two M84 stun grenades.

She grabbed one from her harness, held it in her left hand, and pulled the pin with her right, which still held her pistol. She lobbed the grenade over the two vehicles, aiming for a point just behind the concealed shooter. Even as the grenade arced through the air, Amira dashed around the back of her vehicle towards the rear of the rebel's Hilux, firing the SIGSAUER as she moved.

Her bullets were intended as a diversion, shattering the other Hilux's windows. The rebel remained crouched throughout the barrage, unaware of the stun grenade that had landed four feet behind him. The grenade detonated with a tremendous explosion and a flash of light that deafened and blinded him. He fell over and screamed in pain but couldn't hear himself through the buzzing in his head.

Amira rounded the vehicle, stalked over to where the last rebel lay on his side, his AK-47 no longer in his grasp. *Worked like a charm,* Amira thought, and struck the downed man hard in the temple. He slumped forwards, the fight over.

She looked around, surveyed the surrounding landscape, and still saw no vehicles in any direction, only random lights from various homes far off. *Good. Time to get to work.*

Chapter 15

Amira stared down at the two incapacitated men who both lay against the large boulder, side by side. *Time to wake them up, unfortunately for one of them.*

As soon as she'd knocked the last rebel unconscious, she'd zip-tied his hands and feet and thrown him with some effort into the back of the rebel's Hilux. The man she'd struck with the car had suffered a broken right leg, a shattered hip, and possible internal injuries, but she'd secured and placed him in the SUV's trunk area. She'd driven her vehicle fifty yards off the road, parked it, and taken the keys with her, knowing she'd be back once she was done. It was drivable, and she still had to retrieve her backpack from the northwest corner just outside the pumping station. She'd returned to the rebels' vehicle and driven into the expansive wilderness for more than a minute past her staged vehicle. The location was isolated, and a large boulder blocked the road a half a mile away. No one would hear them, which was the point.

She turned on the powerful Surefire flashlight she kept in a small canvas holster, widened the beam, and placed it against the boulder, illuminating the area in a cone of warm, white light.

Amira nudged the injured man's shattered hip, and a groan escaped his lips. She kicked slightly harder, and his eyes fluttered open. One last hard tap elicited a low cry of pain as the wounded man looked at her. "Good. There's one last thing I have to do, and I wanted you to be awake for it. I hope you speak English or at least understand it." Considering one of the official languages of Sudan was English, she figured there was a good chance.

"I...do," the man replied, his voice thick with pain and fatigue. "What...do you want?"

Amira ignored him and turned her attention to the other rebel. He was awake and staring at her with pure hatred, his eyes burning into hers. *At least my eyes are the only things he can see,* as she'd left her neoprene mask on for the work ahead.

"I see you're awake. Good. We can begin."

Both men suddenly recognized the two items Amira held, and their eyes widened in surprise.

"I know. It's a fascinating weapon," Amira said, holding up in her left hand the machete she'd found in the back of the rebel's Hilux. "It can kill, maim, and terrorize. I once read that hundreds of thousands of people have been slaughtered on this continent with this. It's why you chose it, because it terrifies people, makes them easier to control. And this one, well, this one is *sharp,* which is perfect."

"How so?" asked the uninjured rebel.

Amira smiled, although the two men only saw her pale blue eyes sparkling in the artificial light. "Because this is for one of you, as is this," she replied, holding up the suppressed SIGSAUER 9mm pistol. "I won't lie to you – only one of you is walking – well, not necessarily walking – out of here."

"What do you want?" the uninjured man asked.

"Me? I don't want anything. Personally, I'd like to shoot you both. God knows what horrors you've committed and how much innocent blood you've spilled. You killed four guards in your little assault yesterday, and a hostage was killed in the barracks by your men, who all died badly, by the way, either by my hand or the hyenas. That was something, I have to admit. But me? I don't want anything."

"Then why do this?"

Amira moved back as if perplexed by the question. "Because this is what I do. Because you're the bad guy, and I'm the good guy sent to stop you. It's all very simple. Now, listen to me very carefully. You attacked the wrong facility. You should've never shut down the oil supply. It was very short-sighted of you, but you're a self-proclaimed freedom fighter, I'm sure. You bastards never really think things through on the macro level. And for that, you're going to pay the ultimate price."

"Oil? You're an American," the man spat back. "It's *always* about the oil with you people. How much blood have you spilled in the Middle East over it? You're no different than me, no matter what you say."

Amira knew he had a point. "You're not totally wrong, but I don't make policy. I just carry it out on a very tactical level. But it's irrelevant. Here's the bottom line: one of you is going to die right now, and because you're in much better shape than your friend, here, I'm going to leave it up to you to decide."

Amira watched the dawning horror on the man's face as he realized the unthinkable decision she'd just placed in his hands. "You can't," he said, his voice suddenly acidic with hate. "Asim and I grew up together as brothers. Kill us both. I'd rather die."

"It's okay, Omar," Asim said. "You should…carry on…the cause."

They were the last words Asim spoke, as Amira quickly raised the SIGSAUER and shot him in the forehead from only a few feet away. The loud bark of the suppressed pistol felt magnified in the darkness, and Omar screamed in anguish, an honest, mournful cry that made Amira feel slightly guilty about what she'd just done. *Don't. These men are monsters. God knows how many lives they've taken. This is justice. Real, hard, African justice.*

"You…bitch," Omar said, tears streaking down his face.

"You didn't want to make a choice. So I made it for you. And now, it's your turn," Amira said coldly, holstering the pistol.

Amira bent down and deftly rolled him over, his hands and feet secure. He struggled and squirmed on his stomach, cursing her, but she ignored it. An expert in judo, she mounted his lower back and easily manipulated his body with her strong legs. She bent down and whispered into his right ear, "Put your hands over your head, or I'm going to use this machete to cut your throat."

Omar continued to buck beneath her but realized quickly he had no leverage. He stopped struggling, and said, "You're going to burn for this."

"Maybe, but I'd like to think that if either one of us is going to burn for our sins, it's you. Now, place your arms over your head, slowly."

Omar rolled slightly to his right and removed his arms from under his chest, rotating his shoulders until his secured hands stretched out above him.

Amira grabbed his hands and placed them on a large, flat rock. He tried to keep his hands balled into fists, but she slammed the butt of the machete into the back of his hand, not hard enough to break bones but hard enough to reflexively cause his fist to open. She grabbed his left ring and pinky fingers in her left hand.

"I have to know," Amira said in a low voice, taunting him, "how many people have you killed with this blade? It's sharp, cared for, the way I care for my stilettos. I see a few dark spots on the leather handle. No doubt that's blood. I dread to think whose."

Omar remained silent, which was an admission of guilt in Amira's eyes.

"That's what I thought. Monsters like you never acknowledge their misdeeds. You're nothing but a criminal and a coward," Amira said, baiting him.

"Coward?" Omar spat out from beneath her, his face in the dirt. "I've killed more people with that weapon than you can imagine, and *every one* of them deserved it." His voice rang true with self-delusion, justifying the horrors for which he was responsible.

"You know, I thought you'd say something like that," Amira said, quickly extending his two fingers flat on the rock. "And I'm really glad you did."

"Why is that?" Omar asked, confused.

"Because then I don't feel so badly about this," Amira replied, and brought the machete swiftly and forcefully down.

Chapter 16

Paolich Airport, Southern Sudan
0623 Local Time

The dim morning light increased in intensity as Amira Cerone walked back across the runway of the Paolich Airport towards the camp the USAID workers had established. She'd driven back towards the pumping facility, abandoned the Hilux outside the north perimeter, retrieved her backpack, changed clothes, and begun the several-mile hike back to camp. Her adrenaline from the firefights and mission accomplishment had energized her for the long walk. She'd contemplated her final conversation with Omar, her only regret that her leadership wanted him alive.

"You know, you're lucky. If it were up to me, you'd be in the afterlife with your friend," Amira had said as she'd thrown some QuickClot on the stubs at the first joints of his two fingers and bandaged them. "But you're a message, and I need you to understand that. But even if *you* don't get it, I'm sure others will."

"And what is that?" Omar had asked, cradling his mutilated left hand in his right, his wrists still zip-tied together.

"That you should've never taken the pumping station, that you should've let the referendum play out next month. South Sudan will get its independence. Everyone knows it. Your soon-to-be country didn't *need* you, no matter what your ego thinks. It will be here soon enough, and this is the critical part – if you or any other group decide to attack that or any other pumping station, it won't be just me that comes next time. It will be a whole lot of people *just like me or worse,* and no matter what you think, it won't end well for you or anyone like you." She'd knelt down to emphasize her last words, her pale blue eyes boring into his. "Your fight is over, and you survived. For your sake, although I'm not sure you deserve it, I hope you understand that you get a second chance, which is more than the rest of your friends can say."

He'd remained quiet, and she'd abruptly stood, turned, and walked away. She'd left the machete near his damaged Hilux and figured that it would take him a decent amount of time to hop or crawl to it, cut himself free, and escape back under whatever rock from which he'd emerged.

As Trevor would've said, "A job well done. Mission accomplished, and you walked out alive. That's all you can ask for in this business." And she knew he was right. She'd done what her country had asked of her, what they'd trained her to do, but more importantly, what she'd *volunteered* for. The path she walked was the one she'd chosen, and she had no regrets about her choices, including executing the wounded rebel. He hadn't been an innocent. They *all* had blood on their hands.

She crossed to the other side of the runway when a male figure emerged from the main tent. As she neared him, she recognized Dr. David Granger, the US Embassy doctor, a six-foot, handsome man who wore his hair in a care-free, adult version of Justin Bieber.

94

"Amira, what brings you out this early?" he asked, holding a cup of coffee in a white, plastic embassy mug.

"I couldn't sleep. Thought I'd go for a hike. Been gone about forty-five minutes or so, just around the airport. Kind of refreshing, to be honest."

David nodded. "See anything exciting?"

"Exciting? No. Just the sun starting to wake up. Oh. And a hyena. Off in the distance. Why do you ask?"

"One of the security guards came and roused me from my slumber. You know the pumping station that was attacked yesterday a few miles from here?"

"Of course," Amira replied, her pulse racing at the question. The entire team had been briefed on the assault the evening before, hours before she'd been activated to resolve it.

"Well, apparently, there was some kind of attack or rescue operation. I didn't get all the details. They're not clear, but he told me that the hostages are all safe, and all the rebels are dead. Sounds like a battle of some sort."

Amira sounded surprised. "God. That sounds intense. I'm glad the workers are okay, though."

"Exactly. I offered to help if they had any serious injuries, but apparently, the only injuries sustained were fatal ones to the rebels."

"Well, that's something, for sure. And if nothing else, it leaves you to focus on the people in the village today."

"Now *that* is the truth. Okay. I'm going to grab a bite to eat. I suggest you do the same. It's going to be a long day."

Amira smiled, a gesture that made men blush due to her beautiful, exotic features. "Every day in Africa is a long day. Let's get to work."

Part III – Full Circle

Chapter 17

Gaylord National Hotel

The Present

1550 EST

Amira stared at Omar Bol, the leader of the rebel group whose two fingers she'd taken as a message to others in southern Sudan. *I knew I should've killed him.* Her instincts had been to finish the job, but the powers-that-be at Langley had wanted him alive. And now he was in the United States, involved in a plot to assassinate the director of the CIA. *Hindsight is worse than twenty-twenty. It's sometimes a fatal shot right between the running lights.*

"The look on your face is priceless. It's almost what I anticipated. Almost. I've found that the thing anticipated never really lives up to the anticipation itself. I told you you'd burn for what you did to me, and while I won't be setting you on fire – not because I don't want to, mind you – your death will be good enough for me." The hatred she'd seen in those eyes back in Sudan still burned brightly.

She considered a response, but instead, turned her attention to Nafisa, who stood behind Omar. "I know who this one is," Amira said, nodding her head at Omar while avoiding eye contact, "but what does that make you? How do you fit into this madness?"

Omar spoke in reply. "Nafisa, you haven't told her, have you? I thought that would've been the first thing you did."

"I didn't want her to know until it was time, until just before I pulled the trigger," the bitter Nafisa said.

"I understand," Omar said, and dropped it.

But the exchange between the two had triggered an epiphany, and Amira spoke. "Your husband or your brother?"

Nafisa stared at her, spitting words in reply. "What did you say to me?"

"I *said*, 'Your husband or your brother?' That's the only reason you'd have that much hatred for me. The wounded man I killed, Omar's partner, he must've been your husband or your brother, to have that much anger – trust me; I would know." She considered the choice, and said, "I'm guessing husband."

Nafisa's demeanor intensified so sharply that Amira thought the woman might spontaneously combust. For a brief moment, Amira expected an attack, vicious and fast like the first strike, but none came, and the woman turned and left the room.

Omar studied Amira, shaking his head as if chiding an insolent child. "Husband. Asim, the man you executed – not just killed; don't diminish your true crime – was her husband. It's why she gets the pleasure of you killing you once we give her the green light. She deserves her vengeance."

"And what's this green light? Sounds complicated," Amira asked sarcastically.

Omar ignored the comment. "After your Director Tooney is dead. It's actually pretty simple. He dies; then you die; and we all escape as your authorities try to sort it all out."

"Nothing about this seems simple, but what do I know? I'm tied to a chair."

"Yes. You are, and that's where you're going to stay until the very end."

Samuel entered the room. He placed a hand on Omar's left shoulder, and said, "It's time."

"I just have one last question, a last request, so to speak," Amira said.

Samuel raised his eyebrows.

"No. Not for you," Amira said, redirecting her gaze to Omar. "For him."

Omar studied the woman who'd tormented and tortured him, who'd ruined his plans, who'd maimed him. *See what she wants. She's going to die soon, anyhow.* "What is it?"

"How did you get wrapped up in all of this? That's what I don't understand. Someone had to find you to get you involved. You didn't get here on your own."

Omar smiled, knowingly. "I have you to thank for that."

Amira's brow furrowed, perplexed. "I don't understand."

"I know, but they said you would once I tell you this," Omar continued, sending a chill up Amira's spine. "About a year after your attack, a Chinese man came to my village. He told me he worked for the Chinese government, and he offered me a chance for revenge. Several months after we achieved independence, the Chinese National Petroleum Company assumed control from Petrodar over the pumping station. I guess it had something to do with a small war you and your friends waged on the Chinese in Sudan. Rather than side with the US, both Sudan and my South Sudan reached a deal with China over that new oil field."

Amira's head hurt from the implications. *All that blood in Sudan, and yet it's still not over.*

"But unlike Petrodar, the Chinese understood that they needed to take care of the villagers in Paolich. Food, medical supplies, and money poured into the local area. The Chinese even provided engineers to help build a school, something we'd never had. But the Chinese also have long memories, and they offered me a chance to reclaim my honor."

"Is executing a woman tied to a chair honorable?" Amira asked.

"How is it any different from what you did to Asim?" Omar laughed. "Your arrogance is your undoing. You really don't see your hypocrisy."

As much as it psychologically pained her, she knew he had a point. *It's all a matter of perspective.*

"The Chinese are tired of the US meddling in Africa, where they've invested billions of dollars. Within ten years, the Chinese economy will be the dominant global economy, especially if they

101

can get the US to stop playing in their backyard. As a result, they've funded my revenge, pure and simple." He stood before her, his hands held wide, indicating there was nothing else left to say.

"You know it's not going to work, right? No matter what they told you, how much they paid you, what they gave you, it won't work. It never does. My government always finds out the truth, even if they hide it themselves sometimes."

"We'll see, but one thing is for certain – in less than twenty minutes, you'll be dead, and Asim will be avenged. Goodbye."

He abruptly turned and left the room, leaving Amira alone with her spinning thoughts. *Please, God. Let there be a way out. But if not, let me face my fate bravely.*

Less than a minute later, the door to the suite opened and closed one last time, and Amira was left alone with the woman whose husband she'd executed.

Nafisa entered the bedroom and sat down on the edge of the queen bed to Amira's right, her back to Amira. "Finally, we're alone. I can't tell you how long I've waited for this."

That makes one of us, Amira thought, counting down the seconds in her mind, praying for help she knew wasn't coming.

Chapter 18

The two women sat in silence for several minutes, which suited Amira as she mentally counted down the clock ticks left in her life. *You can't blame her. You killed her husband. She's doing what you would've done, what you have done. But you also know she's blinded by her hatred. She's about to throw her life away because after today, if they succeed, they'll find and kill her.* Of that, Amira was certain. Once she was dead, John would hunt Nafisa down literally to the ends of the earth. There'd be no place safe from the wrath of Amira's lover. *Give her a chance.*

"I understand why you hate me. Believe me. I get it, but are you really willing to throw away your life? Because that's what you're doing. Omar is a monster. I knew that the night I met him, but I barely had a moment with your husband. Did Omar tell you the full story of how Asim died?"

Amira *felt* the loathing, but she prayed there was a glimpse of reason left.

Nafisa turned on the edge, her legs in the space between the two beds, and looked at Amira. When she spoke, her words were quiet, as if by speaking softly they could counteract the fury behind them. "He said you shot him in the head, that you never gave him a chance. That *you* ambushed them as they fled, caused an accident, and captured them both alive, only to *murder* my husband."

That sonofabitch. He lied to her, at least partially. You have to get to her to see the truth. Amira edged forward slightly, the subtle movement intended to emphasize her sincerity. "Nafisa, I know you despise me, and I know you have no reason to believe me, but what I'm about to tell you is the truth, the *entire* truth. Yes. I killed your husband. Yes. I shot him in the head. That part is true. But I shot him because I thought he was already dying from his injuries, and I needed one of them alive because that was part of my mission. I swear to God."

Nafisa stared at her, and then her eyes squinted slightly, a flicker of something *other* than unadulterated hatred. "What injuries?"

For the first time of the day, Amira felt a glimmer of hope. *There's a chance, small, but now it's there. Take it.* "I'm not surprised he didn't tell you. He's a monster, Nafisa. A very real, evil monster. He doesn't care about you. He's just using you because that's what he does."

Amira witnessed the impact of the words, like invisible punches that made it through Nafisa's defenses.

"I *said,* 'What injuries?'"

"It wasn't I who ambushed them," Amira said, pausing for effect. "They stopped their pick-up in the middle of the road and opened fire on me. I did the only thing I could – I floored it and

104

struck the driver, who was still shooting at me when I did. Turns out that was your husband. I swear to you, I thought I killed him when I hit him. I then used a stun grenade to subdue Omar, who was relatively uninjured." Amira paused again. "I can see that he didn't tell you any of this. It's written all over your face, like your hatred for me."

Nafisa didn't reply, but she adjusted herself on the bed. The suppressed Glock in her right hand lay on her thigh, the muzzle still pointed at Amira.

"I had a choice to make – your husband or Omar. Omar was the leader, and your husband, I thought he was dying of internal injuries. He was in bad shape. I was shocked he'd survived." Amira let the words sink in, knowing she had one last card to play. "You know, I gave Omar a choice – him or Asim. And you know what he said?"

A pained expression appeared on Nafisa's face, softening the mask of hatred.

She's on the ropes. Finish her. It's your only chance. "He said he'd rather die. He didn't try to plea for Asim's life. He refused to make the choice. And do you know why? Because the only thing a man like Omar cares about is his so-called cause. He's a true believer, but that makes everyone around him expendable, including your husband." Amira stopped speaking, the truth hanging in the air between them.

Nafisa's face was a portrait of pure torment, her hatred and anguish battling each other across the features of her beautiful face.

Amira sat in silence as the struggle unfolded. *She has to reach the conclusion herself. It's the only way.*

Nafisa suddenly ceased moving, the transformation complete, her eyes fixed on the carpet in front of Amira's feet. "I told him Omar would get him killed. I knew the day would come. I *tried* to save him." Nafisa looked up into Amira's face, the pain and anguish now the prominent emotions displayed. "But he wouldn't listen. They were best friends since they were little, inseparable. Unlike Omar, Asim was kind, gentle. He wanted to help people. He always did, but the idea of a free South Sudan was always the most important thing to Omar, and I told Asim, but he just...wouldn't...listen."

Amira gave her ten seconds to compose herself, and then spoke. "Nafisa, I am sorry for your loss. Truly. But if you don't help me, many more people are going to die today because of Omar. If what you say about your husband is true, he wouldn't want you to do this, to throw your life away for Omar. Please. Help me."

The plea hung suspended between them, and Amira waited, the tension increasing by the moment. She could feel Nafisa's desire to help, but something still held her back. *You're running out of time.*

Nafisa looked into Amira's face, a resolve set where none had been moments before. "But *you* still killed him. And I can't forgive that, no matter how much I try. My husband was a good man, a strong man, but I'm not my husband."

106

There's your answer. Amira knew some people weren't capable of forgiveness, even when they knew the alternative was self-destruction and damnation. Nafisa's grief had been too much for her to bear. Amira saw it clearly, and she knew her fate had been sealed long ago. But she had to try, for Director Tooney, for herself, and most importantly, for John.

"Don't do this. It's *wrong,* and you know it," Amira stated.

A knock at the door interrupted Nafisa before she could respond. She looked at her watch and then at Amira. "Only a few more minutes," she said, and rose from the bed, her composure that of a woman once again in control.

"You still have time to save yourself."

Nafisa stopped in the doorway and glanced back, resignation the sole expression left on her face. "No. It's too late for me…and *for you.*"

Amira's last hope faded as Nafisa disappeared into the other room. She was out of options, frustration and hopelessness threatening to set in and drag her into the next life. *No,* her father said inside her head. *There's always a way. Right up to the end.* She knew he was right, and she steeled herself. She would not cower in fear, even if it was her end.

She twisted her hands in a failed attempt to break the zip-tie behind the back of the chair, a rectangular, narrow cushion with a wooden frame. She rocked the chair to the side in an attempt to topple it, but the queen bed stopped her momentum. *There's not enough space between the beds to get you on the floor.* She had to figure out a way to turn the chair ninety degrees in the confined space and then knock it over, but she knew Nafisa would be back before she succeeded. *You have to try, for John, for your father, for yourself.*

There was a muffled voice from outside the room, and Nafisa replied, "I'm sorry, but I don't need service today. The sign is up."

A second reply came back through the door, words Amira couldn't understand. *Housekeeping. Keep talking. I need more time,* she thought desperately. She struggled to turn the chair, lifting up and down but unable to get the leverage she needed from the floor. *This isn't working.*

"It must have fallen off. I don't really know, but either way, we're good for today. Thank you."

Those were the last words Nafisa spoke as the door exploded inwards and the glass from the balcony door in the living room shattered. Nafisa was flung backwards several feet as the edge of the door caught her in the right shoulder. She stumbled sideways deeper into the suite but kept herself upright, the suppressed Glock still in her right hand. She regained her footing as she came face-to-face with a fearsome looking man in a dark sweater, khakis, and bright green eyes that danced with a righteous fury aimed directly at her. *He's some kind of devil,* she thought. *And he's come for me.*

"Drop it!" the man ordered, a pistol aimed directly at Nafisa.

Nafisa heard movement behind her, and she realized her moment had arrived – her life was over. *But I'm not going alone. I have to avenge Asim,* she thought, and swung her arm towards the object of her hatred and rage – Amira.

Amira watched in horror, as if in slow motion, through the doorway as Nafisa's arm came up. *I'm sorry, John. I tried. I love you,* she thought, cleared her mind, and fixed her eyes on her executioner's. She would face her death like a warrior, without apology.

A single suppressed gunshot rang out from the living room and struck Nafisa in the chest just left of center a split-second before she pulled the trigger on the suppressed Glock. The impact from the unseen shooter's bullet knocked her aim off-center as she was spun to her left by the pain, and the round went wide, shattering the lamp on the nightstand behind Amira.

Amira flinched at the destruction behind her, but she kept her eyes fixed on Nafisa's as her would-be killer collapsed on her side to the carpeted floor as if curling up for an afternoon nap. Blood spread quickly from the wound, soaking and darkening her shirt.

Shouts emanated from both sides of the doorway, but neither woman heard them, as each was fixed on the other.

She's dying. She's got seconds left, Amira thought, and was somehow filled with a sadness for the woman who'd tried to kill her in the last moments of her life. "I'm sorry. It didn't have to be this way."

Nafisa eye's bored into Amira's. "Yes…it did," she said faintly as blood poured from her mouth. Her eyes dropped to the floor, her head suspended several inches above the carpet.

So much loss, Amira thought and closed her eyes. *So much.*

"Clear!" she heard two men say in unison in the living room, and she recognized each voice, relief pouring over her as her eyes shot open.

"In here!"

Two men appeared in the doorway, but her eyes locked on the shorter of the two, a fit, rugged, handsome man with a short haircut and a look of concern that struck Amira like a punch. *John Quick. My love.*

Amira tried to speak but was overwhelmed with relief, and she reflexively stopped herself from breaking down, her body shaking with the effort.

John rushed forward and yanked a small black knife out of a Velcro sheath on his belt. He pressed the button, and the blade shot out, ready to work. "It's okay. We've got you. You're safe, now. *I've* got you." His voice was thick with emotion as he wrapped his arms around her, comforting her.

Amira welcomed the embrace and buried her head into his shoulder. She struggled to speak, and she forced herself to regain her composure. "I love you," she whispered. "I love you so much."

She felt the zip-tie break behind her, and her arms were suddenly free. She wrapped them around John and squeezed, cherishing the moment, as she knew it wouldn't last.

"I love you, too," John replied, moving back and gripping the sides of her face. "Always."

"I know," Amira said, her eyes glistening but not relinquishing the tears that lingered there. She smiled, and for one brief moment, all felt right in the world, even as Nafisa's blood stained the carpet behind them. "But we have to move. They're trying to assassinate Director Tooney, and we're almost out of time."

"Who is?" the human force of nature known as Logan West asked as he stood watching the two people that he loved dearly as friends and fellow members of Task Force Ares.

Amira stood up, unsteady for a moment, but pushed John's arms away. "I've got this."

"Don't I know it," John said, a hint of his natural sarcasm back in his voice.

"I'm pretty sure it's the Chinese, and it's all because of what happened in Sudan, what I did *before* we met. We need to get downstairs to the convention center. I'll fill you in on the way down, but Logan, you need to call Tooney and tell him he's in imminent danger out there in the Riverview Ballroom, as in right now, and then, you two can tell me how you tracked me. There's a conference, and he's a keynote speaker about to talk, and once he starts, they're going to kill him."

"On it," Logan said, and slid out his encrypted iPhone from his back pocket.

A third man, a tall, good-looking white male with a shock of gray hair in his fifties appeared from around the corner, staring in bewilderment at the death that had occurred inside the room.

Amira nodded. "Who's that?"

"That?" John said, smiling, "that's Chris Hauty, and he's the head of security for the Gaylord. You owe him dinner, babe, as he's the one who helped us locate you."

"In that case," Amira said, smiling, her pale blue eyes flashing, "it's nice to meet you. Now, can someone please get me a gun? We've got work to do."

Chapter 19

As the glass elevator descended, Amira studied the lower
atrium and fountain nineteen stories below. The impressive
cavernous space left most first-time visitors awestruck at the scale of
the hotel and the atrium. The elevator in which they rode was on the
south wing of the hotel, which was a typical u-shaped building with
two tiers on each wing. The first part that extended out from each
side of the main building had nineteen-floors, but then two lower
additions – like arms reaching out towards the Potomac River – had
seven floors each. With two thousand guest rooms, the architects
had applied their creative genius and enclosed the first nineteen-
floor space with a glass wall that rose up from the roof of the lower
sections at the end of each wing and connected to a curved glass
roof. Similarly, at the end of the lower sections, another glass wall
covered by a second curved glass roof stood as the final barrier to
the outside. The construction created an enormous glass and girder
bubble, and it drew visitors who ate, shopped, and gawked at the
architectural feat.

Hundreds of people moved over the walkways, in between
shops, under the indoor trees, and around the fountain, soaking in
the atmosphere and the holiday decorations the Gaylord had already

put up. *So many people. What a nightmare. There's no way to spot anyone in this crowd.*

"You reach Tooney?" Amira asked Logan. Logan, John, and Amira held their suppressed pistols beneath open jackets.

"Negative, but I reached Jake, and he's reaching out to Langley to see if they can contact the director's personal security detail. And Chris here has already radioed the hotel security manning the entrance to the Riverview Ballroom, which is where the summit is. Tooney should be in there somewhere, getting ready to talk. His detail should be able to handle any threat."

"You don't get it – there's someone in there who looks like me who's going to use my identity to get close to him, and no matter how good they are, they won't stop her. We all know that. Also, Emerson said that his contacts were in the hotel's security. You may have just let the bad guys know we're on the way. Let's just pray we get there in time." Amira had reclaimed her iPhone from the hotel room – where her abductors had removed her SIM card and turned off her phone – and she checked the time. "We have four minutes." She placed it back in the black Oakley daypack they'd taken, as well. Some women liked Michael Kors chic; Amira preferred Oakley tactical.

The glass elevator continued to descend, steel girders passing by with each floor.

"How did you find me? And make it quick."

"Yes, ma'am," John said. "When you didn't respond to my texts after lunch, I checked your last location on the Find My app. It

114

showed the garage, and then it disappeared. Considering our line of work, I knew something was wrong. I called Logan, and since Cole is on leave visiting his parents in North Carolina," he said, referring to the former chief of the CIA's Special Activities Division, one-time Delta operator, and fellow core member of Task Force Ares, "the two of us showed up at the National Harbor's private security company's command center. Turns out having FBI badges helps. Security camera footage showed you enter the garage, walk, and disappear into a blind spot. Fifteen seconds later, two men did the same thing. It was the last time you were seen on camera, and they have most of the place covered. The only thing that left within minutes was a white panel van, which cameras tracked to the service entrance to the hotel. We hustled over here, linked up with Chris, and used the hotel's cameras to identify the van in the back. Two men rolled out a laundry cart – with unfolded laundry in it; not what you'd be taking *into* a hotel – and passed it off to a member of the housekeeping staff. We looked at footage of every floor from the service elevators and finally spotted her moving the cart on the nineteenth. When she got to that suite, she entered and left within a minute, and the cart was noticeable lighter. Once we identified the room – which took serious time, looking at all of that footage – we started watching the live stream of that hallway's camera to see who went in and out. We still weren't sure, until we saw a white male with a gun in a concealed holster as he adjusted his jacket. At that point, Logan climbed up from the room below – which I'm sure was a sight, if anyone was paying attention – and I kicked the door in.

Honestly, we weren't sure you were here, but Chris gave me a key card and the green light. Sorry if we cut it close, hon."

"But how did you know there was only one person in there?"

"With this," John said, and pulled out a device from his own backpack. It looked like a dark-green oversized satellite phone, but it had a handle sticking out at an angle from the back and a digital display above the handle. "Borrowed this awhile back from our HRT friends. While it doesn't show pictures of what's inside a room through walls – that non-sense is for Hollywood – it does detect the number of people and approximately how far from the wall or door you place this bad boy on."

Amira nodded, impressed.

The elevator announced their arrival with an audible ding, and the doors slid open.

"You made it. That's *all* that matters." She smiled at him. "And that's some solid police work. You two would've made a good pair of detectives."

John laughed. "Police? Too many rules. Too many so-called rights for the bad guys." He paused, suddenly serious. "Besides, your dad was the best cop I knew, and I could never live up to that."

Amira smiled as the familiar sensation that her father's spirit was with her, a presence she'd felt several times since his death. "None of us can, but we can still try. Let's go."

They stepped out into the roaring noise of people talking, dishes clanging, footsteps, and other background noises that formed one constant stream of sound. Logan, John, and Amira held their pistols – suppressors removed in the elevator – low and wore FBI badges on chains around their necks. Logan had his Kimber Tactical II Pro.45-caliber pistol; John carried his M1911 .45-cal pistol he'd used since his days in the Marine Corps; Amira held her SIGSAUER P229 9mm pistol, a favorite since her days in Africa; and Chris Hauty held the Glock they'd retrieved from Nafisa. As Logan had said, "The more firepower, the better." While he wasn't technically law enforcement, a man trained to use a gun was still a force multiplier.

Chapter 20

Just as Samuel predicted, which means Nafisa is either dead or under arrest. Either way, Omar knew it was now up to him to delay Amira and the three men that accompanied her down the glass elevator. No matter what happened, he would not leave her alive.

Amira and her companions exited the elevator and turned right, moving through the crowd towards the Riverview Ballroom.

"Open fire when I do," Omar said quietly to the private contractor Trevor Emerson had assigned to him.

A disgruntled former Army staff sergeant who'd watched too many of his friends die in Afghanistan, Tony Bernelli's cynicism was complete and unhindered. He'd learned the hard way that the US government didn't care about its service members or its citizens. It was why the five-foot-eleven former Special Forces Green Beret now served only himself and his family. The job was the job, and Trevor Emerson paid well.

"Understood," Tony replied, the weight of his concealed, holstered Glock 17 9mm pistol on his right hip reassuring as he fell in step next to Omar.

The two men followed Amira, deftly weaving in and out of the crowd, closing the distance to their unsuspecting prey. Both parties had passed the stand-alone stores in the middle that resembled village storefronts, and Omar was running out of room. His targets would be near the exit within seconds. He stopped and withdrew the Glock 9mm pistol he'd concealed under his sport coat. He sensed Tony do the same. *Vengeance is mine,* he thought, his mind blocking out the thrum of the crowd and the movement of the people around him.

His focus was completely on Amira and the three men with her. It was also why he failed to hear the scream of a father with his two children and wife ten feet to his left at a table in the open-air section of the main restaurant. Had Omar known the man was a Marine Corps major on leave with his family, he might have reconsidered the point at which he'd stopped. But it was too late, and the man screamed, "GUN!!!" as Omar and Tony raised their weapons.

A second of time hung in the air, as if a gap had been created between the past and the future, the moment when families enjoyed their early dinners, to the moment unfettered chaos broke out and panic raged across the Gaylord National atrium. In that space, confusion reigned as bystanders processed what the warning meant in the age of domestic terrorism. But Amira, Logan, and John weren't civilian bystanders, and the heartbeat that transformed the Gaylord was enough to trigger their reactions, even as Omar and Tony pulled the triggers on their Glocks.

Sensing the threat behind them, Amira and John dove left under the suspended belt held up by stanchions that marked the edge of the restaurant seating area. Logan dove right, twisting in his dive

119

towards the fountain and the enormous Christmas tree within, his Kimber eager to locate the threat.

Without the years of endless and repetitive training, Chris Hauty was the only one who didn't react, which was why he was the one struck in the back by several bullets. He fell forwards to the hard, smooth, stone floor, his consciousness fading as his blood drained from multiple holes. Snapshots of his family, his wife, their children, and young grandchildren appeared in his mind. A devout Catholic, he believed he'd see them again, and he closed his eyes one last time, content in the knowledge as death embraced him.

"Motherfuckers," John said, scrambling under a table as the guests scattered around them. He felt a pang of sorrow at the security chief's murder, but he suppressed it, knowing the time to grieve and honor the dead would come later.

More shots rang out, and they struck tables and chairs that were overturned by the diners' rush to safety.

Amira was sickened at the willful negligence and callous disregard of their attackers, but then she saw Omar, and she knew the truth once again – *he doesn't care about anyone but himself.*

"Logan! Get to the ballroom and stop the attack! We'll cover you! Move!" Amira shouted across the walkway, praying he'd heard her through the chaos as he hunkered down behind the trunk of a large tree.

Both Amira and John knelt behind a table, looked at each other, nodded and stood up in a crouch, their weapons aimed at Omar and a second shooter twenty feet away.

120

Too many people behind them. "Shoot into the ceiling, and I'll flank them. Now." Amira demanded.

John never hesitated, crouched down, and fired the 1911 into the air, which served two purposes – to suppress the two shooters and force the remaining bystanders near the gunfight to fling themselves to the floor. He fired several times, praying the vaulted glass ceiling several stories above wouldn't come crashing down upon all of their heads.

Logan leapt into action at the first shot, sprinting towards the glass wall and the exit to the walkways outside that led to the Riverview Ballroom.

The slide on John's 1911 locked back, the magazine empty. John ducked down, ejected the magazine, inserted another, and pulled the slide, releasing it. He stood up to engage the shooters but held his fire and smiled at the sight of Amira charging the two men from the side. *Get those fuckers, babe.*

===

John's fire had forced Omar and the second shooter to back against the wall of the free-standing convenience store and hide behind a large Christmas tree. Amira had crouched down and skirted along a row of fallen tables until she was behind a plastic Roman architecture support column for the awning of the restaurant, parallel to the shooters.

John's 1911 went silent, and Amira spun around the column, her SIGSAUER at the ready. *Gotcha.*

Omar's little helper was less than fifteen feet away in between her and Omar. He stood back up to return fire when Amira pulled the trigger one time, striking the man in the side of the head. Even as he collapsed to the stone floor, Omar recognized the mortal peril he was suddenly in, and he took a step backwards, turned, and dashed towards the open door to the store.

Amira couldn't risk firing into the building, as she knew the 9mm rounds would easily pass through the thin walls. She sprang into a run and gave chase, covering the open ground in seconds.

Omar was already through the door when he crashed into a man who'd mistakenly thought it would be a good idea to try and get a glimpse of the chaos outside the store. Both Omar and the young man in his late twenties crashed to the store floor and slid into a rack of snacks erected in the middle of the floor. Omar pulled up his right hand to fire into the man's stomach, when he realized with surprise that he'd dropped the Glock. Instead, he punched the man twice in the face, broke his nose, and scrambled backwards, lifting himself to his knees.

He turned back towards the door as the figure of Amira Cerone rushed through the entrance, her pistol trained on him. Omar snarled at the woman he despised purely and completely, grabbed a box of Cliff power bars off the shelf next to him, and flung them at her as he launched himself off his knees towards his enemy. *I won't go down without a fight.*

Amira batted away the projectile power bars, the SIG still in her right hand, as she collided into the attacking, muscular figure of Omar Bol. *I guess we'll do this the hard way.* She sensed several bystanders inside the store, cowering in the corners on the floor, and she feared a stray shot would take an innocent life.

As Omar wrapped his arms around her, his head to the right side of her chest under her arm, she quickly turned her head and flung the SIG through the doorway to the walkway outside, where she knew John would collect it after he secured the scene around the other shooter's body.

The momentary action gave Omar the advantage, and he punched her hard in the left side three times before she could react. Her ribs and abdomen absorbed the blows, and she slammed her right elbow down on to the base of his skull. The blow staggered him, and he released her waist and spun to the left. Amira pressed forward, spun on her left foot, switched to her right foot mid-spin, and struck Omar in the hip with a back kick. The blow sent him careening into a spinning rack of paperback books, and both Omar and the rack tumbled to the floor as the paperbacks fell out of their holders. Omar picked up a book and hurled it in Amira's direction as she stalked towards him.

She easily deflected it, and said, "This *ends* now." As she passed the pentagonal counter in the middle of the floor, she grabbed a silver Gaylord National letter opener from a hanging rack next to the register.

Omar threw another book, and Amira ducked as it sailed past, catching a glimpse of a soldier on the cover, staring into the wilderness over big block letters that read, "OVER WATCH."

Omar rose to his feet, his eyes on the letter opener, and he pulled a short push-dagger from beneath his jacket.

Amira smiled at the appearance of the blade. "Good. I don't want to be accused of killing an unarmed man."

The bystanders gasped at the unfolding knife fight, and several fled through the two entrances into the store.

"Go to hell," Omar said, and threw a left jab at her face with the intention of distracting Amira in order to close the distance.

"You first," Amira said as Omar attacked.

Unfortunately for Omar, Amira Cerone was one of the most skilled hand-to-hand combat fighters in service of the CIA and Task Force Ares, and she identified the feint for what it was. She brought the letter opener up so fast Omar never saw it until it was sticking out of the bottom of his forearm and the pain had blossomed in his arm. She pulled out the letter opener, the blood glistening on the silver blade, and grabbed his right wrist with her left hand, immobilizing the push-dagger.

Amira's eyes blazed with fury as Omar struggled futiley against her grip. "There's nowhere left to run, Omar. Your time has finally come. All you did in Africa was for nothing, only to die in a losing effort on US soil. Now, go to hell, for good."

Before Omar could respond, Amira twisted his right wrist to the left and plunged the letter opener into his left side. She felt the blade grind against a rib as she pushed farther, searching for a vital organ.

Omar shrieked in pain, and his body went rigid as if an electric current ran through it.

Amira mercilessly withdrew the letter opener, released the blade mid-air, and switched her grip with the blade now emerging from the back of her right hand. With blinding speed, she brought the letter opener in front of Omar, and he watched in horror as she buried it into his chest, piercing his heart. He stared down and saw the $19.99 sticker on the handle facing up, looked at Amira one last time. Her merciless pale blue eyes were the last things he saw as the darkness consumed him, and he fell to the shop's floor, dead.

"Are you okay?" John said from behind her, and Amira felt her heart race at the sound of his voice. He held her pistol in his left hand, as she'd known he would.

She turned and faced him, and said, "The world is a better place with this monster no longer in it. I'll tell you the whole story after this nightmare is over."

"That's my girl," John said, and smiled. "Now, let's go help Logan before he destroys this place. Minus the gunfight, I kind of like it and wouldn't mind coming back."

Amira smiled at her lover's morbid sarcasm. "One thing at a time, killer. Let's go."

John handed her the SIGSAUER pistol, and the two dashed out of the store in pursuit of Logan, hoping there was still time to save Director Tooney.

Chapter 21

Logan West ran down the concrete walkway from the atrium to the Riverview Ballroom, which had been constructed off-set to the right of the Gaylord and closer to the Potomac River in order to create the capital region's first infinity ballroom. The sun was still up and wouldn't set for another twenty minutes or so, but the wind blew in off the water, swirling around him as he ran, although the Kevlar vest he wore kept him warm.

The day had started like most others after the events in Venezuela earlier in the year – Sarah and he had changed and fed Sophia, who at three and a half months, had finally started sleeping through the night. He'd thought endless days of sleep deprivation at the Marine Corps Basic Reconnaissance Course and then years of training in Force Reconnaissance Company had prepared him for fatherhood, but he was still tired, day after day, although he knew Sarah carried most of the burden. After the morning routine, he'd checked in with Jake Benson, the unofficial overseer of Task Force Ares, as dictated by President Preston Scott. But after Venezuela and the dismantling of the Organization, the task force had laid low, checking in at their new headquarters on the grounds of Quantico co-located with the FBI's Hostage Rescue Team, headed by their close friend and ally, Lance Foster. But then John had called him at home, and the day had escalated wildly, until once again, Logan found himself running with a gun towards a new threat. *Can't catch a break.*

More gunshots erupted behind him in the atrium, but he ignored them and prayed his friends were on the giving end of the gunfire.

He reached the first set of doors to the Riverview lobby and yanked the one on the right wide open.

The Riverview Ballroom was a two-story, rectangular structure with a curved roof that dipped down where the lobby emptied into the enormous sixteen-thousand-square-foot ballroom enclosed by glass on three sides that overlooked the Potomac River and DC to the east. The panoramic vistas were breathtaking, and the venue was usually booked a year in advance.

He stepped into the lobby, which ran the length of the facility. On the right were the restrooms and a series of rooms that comprised the pantry and kitchen to stage the food for the events held in the ballrom.

On the left, a series of doors were set at intervals along the entire lobby, providing access to the ballroom. The doors were all open, as attendees of the summit moved back and forth between the main venue and the lobby. *Great. More crowds. What did you expect? This is the Big Leagues when it comes to the Intelligence Community.*

Several people stopped mid-stride as Logan stalked across the blue carpet towards the first set of open doors, his Kimber at the ready and the FBI badge swinging across his chest. Their civilian senses told them something was amiss, but they weren't sure what, although Logan was certain had they known, they would've fled in a panic. *Keep the panic to a minimum, until it's out of the bag.*

Screams and a series of gunshots reverberated from inside the ballroom, and Logan sprinted to the doors, hoping to get through them before the bystanders inside fled for their lives. *Well, so much for the element of surprise.*

Logan burst into the ballroom and stepped to the left along the wall besides the door as the first panic-stricken people dashed out of the line of fire past him. What had been a speech on the cyber vulnerabilities of America's power grid, specifically, the supervisory control and data acquisition systems – known as SCADA – that controlled it, had turned into a sustained gunfight.

Logan West absorbed the entire scene in an instant and snapped a mental picture, even as he moved left along the wall. Director Tooney was nowhere in sight, but three of his personal security detail crouched behind the elevated stage on which the director had been speaking. Large, cushioned chairs had been knocked over, providing additional cover to the men behind the stage. A fourth agent lay on the stage, unmoving, blood pooling around his still body. The three protective agents were engaged in a gun battle on two fronts, and he recognized Charlie Jenkins, the head of the director's detail, as he'd met the man on multiple occasions.

Two hostile shooters, a man and a woman – Amira's double, Logan realized – stood near the left glass wall while two others fired

128

from the far side of the ballroom. And all four concentrated their fire towards the podium and the protective detail behind it.

The only good thing in Logan's mind was that the bad guys were using pistols, probably because it was easier to conceal a pistol than a long gun. But that didn't matter to the several hundred people trapped inside when the gun battle began – they knocked over audience chairs and scrambled for safety towards the back of the ballroom.

Need to even the odds. Logan moved against the tide of humanity along the back wall until he reached the glass windows on the left side of the ballroom. The sound of gunfire combined with the screams of the bystanders was deafening inside the enclosed space. Bullet holes appeared in all three walls, and Logan was reminded of the battle at the mountaintop hotel in Venezuela ten months ago. *Why is there always so much glass?* He kept moving forward.

He was twenty-five feet away, and both shooters' backs were to him. The Kimber was up and locked on the back of the head of the male shooter, who was closest to him. Unfortunately, several people still fled towards him, as if the side of the ballroom could somehow grant them refuge. A woman spotted him from ten feet away and screamed in horror, mistaking him for one of the attackers. He grabbed his badge with his left hand, pulled it away from his chest to show her and the others who'd seen him, and motioned for them all to get down.

The second it took for her and the attendees near her to process and follow his instructions was enough to gain the attention of the man he'd locked on to with his Kimber's front sight. As they dropped to the carpet, the man turned to see what had caused the commotion, and he spotted Logan just in time to see the bearer of his death.

Logan pulled the trigger, and the Kimber *roared* inside the space, and the jacketed hollow point struck the man in the right eye, blowing out the back of his head and spraying the Amira look-a-like with a dark red mist. *That got her attention, I'm sure.*

She stopped firing towards the back of the ballroom and turned towards Logan, the right side of her face and head covered in blood. Her eyes were wide as she saw the man who'd pulled the trigger. She screamed in outrage and swept the muzzle of the pistol towards Logan. She made it halfway before Logan pulled the trigger once again.

The round struck her just above the right eye, and she dropped to the carpet, no longer a threat to anyone in the land of the living.

The gun battle on the right side of the ballroom continued, the two attackers unaware of the fate of their two friends on the opposite side.

Logan glanced at the stage and spotted Charlie Jenkins staring at him, recognition and relief written upon his face. Logan pointed through the fleeing masses towards the other two shooters and received a nod from the head of the director's detail. *Now, for the really fun part.*

He crouched low and began to combat walk quickly through the crowd, weaving in and out of moving bodies. He was confident in his approach, as he knew the shooters' goal wasn't to slaughter innocent civilians but to assassinate the director of the CIA. While he knew that key piece of information, the crowd didn't, which explained the chaos and panic that reigned in the ballroom.

The director's detail concentrated their fire on the far side of the room, striking the glass behind the shooters and a rolling drink tray they used for cover. Bullets bounced off the tray, and Logan realized they'd added some kind of bulletproofing to it under the white cloth that covered it. *Smart bastards.*

He was halfway across the room, and most of the crowd had reached the back half of the ballroom like an amoeba moving across a petri dish. In a few more seconds, he'd lose his concealment, and he prepared to take his shots the second he was exposed.

A few more feet, and the last attendees cleared the area around him like a living fog dissipating. Logan stopped, raised the Kimber, and placed the front sight on the torso of the man on the right. At forty feet, the Kimber Tactical II was accurate, but it was still a precision shot. He slowly squeezed the trigger, and the .45-caliber roared in his hand, the heavy barrel recoiling. He didn't wait to see the impact of his round, and he squeezed the trigger two more times until he saw one of the bullets strike the man in the upper chest just below his neck. The shooter reflexively dropped his pistol and clutched at the hole in his upper torso as blood flowed over his fingers. He stood for a moment and looked around as if hoping someone might come to his aid, and then he fell forward on top of the cart.

Logan ignored the dramatic display and adjusted the Kimber to the second shooter, who began to turn in his direction.

An explosion of pain struck his right side as if he'd been hit with a baseball bat, and he collapsed to his knees on the carpet, his Kimber still in his right hand. He struggled for breath, the pain excruciating, and he knew he'd been hit. *Should've assumed they had a back-up team.* He turned his head to the right and saw three men – a white, middle-aged man with black hair; a lanky black man who looked like he was from the same country in Africa as the woman in the hotel room; and a third white male dressed like the hotel staff – pointing weapons at him, although their line of sight had mercifully been obstructed once again by the last few attendees trying to escape.

Logan tried to raise his Kimber, but like a boxer temporarily incapacitated from a punch to his liver, his arm wouldn't function, and he fell to his left side, facing his soon-to-be executioners. *This should not be how this ends,* he thought. He closed his eyes, pictured his wife and daughter, holding them both in the rocking chair in Sophia's room, and waited for the end to come.

A barrage of gunfire erupted, and Logan reflexively imagined the bullets striking his body, sending him into the next world. But all he felt was his body begin to respond to his commands to recover from the blow to the Kevlar vest, and he opened his eyes.

The middle-aged man and lanky African had turned to flee, and the third shooter lay face down on the carpet, his head turned with vacant eyes looking at Logan. A neat hole had appeared in the middle of his forehead, and blood oozed from it. Logan smiled at the revelation he was still among the living, and he realized what had happened – Charlie Jenkins and the remainder of the protective agents had opened fire on Logan's attackers. *Thank God.*

Bullets struck the door frame and walls as the two men fled. Logan glanced back at his original target and saw that the second shooter he'd failed to take down had been killed by the protective detail.

He tried to rise to pursue the two men, but he collapsed back to his knees, not yet in full control of his body. His last image was of both the older shooter and thin African turning right. *Bastards are going to get away. Goddamnit.*

He concentrated on his breathing and wondered if he'd sustained one or more cracked ribs, but then he thought of his former close friend and brother-in-arms, Mike Benson, who'd died in a gunfight at a rare earth elements production facility outside of Las Vegas. The bullet had struck him just over the Kevlar vest under his arm, and he had died within minutes, although not before saving the facility and leaving Logan a voicemail that still filled him with love every time he listened to it. *It's not my day to die.*

Several seconds later, he felt a presence behind him and heard Charlie Jenkins' voice. "Your part of this fight is over. Just take it easy."

Logan sat on his haunches, furious that he'd been taken out of the fight. He looked up as Charlie knelt in front of him. "I'm just glad I could help, even a little."

"Logan, killing three bad guys and saving our ass is more than just a 'little.' How's the side? Thank God you wore that thing."

"Tell me about it," Logan said, grimacing as a new jolt of pain raced up his ribs. "How's Tooney? What the hell happened before I joined the fun?"

"I received a call from the agency about the threat thirty seconds before they opened fire. We were moving to the stage to get him when Tom Carmen spotted the first shooter and jumped in front of the director. He took the first several bullets and died doing his job, God rest his soul," Charlie said as a sudden wave of grief flashed across his face at the loss of a fellow agent and close friend. He composed himself and continued. "The director's fine, although he might've broken his left wrist when we threw him to the floor behind the stage."

Logan nodded. "He's a lucky man. And by the way, nice shooting. I owe you one."

"It was the least we could do, considering what you'd just done to get us out of this mess. I have to be honest, I don't know the details, as the director would never tell me, but he considers you almost an equal. I assume you know what this is all about."

The noise had died down substantially, and Logan realized that they were alone with the dead attackers inside the enormous ballroom. He knew the aftermath would be coming soon, with paramedics and law enforcement arriving on the scene within minutes.

"Almost?" Logan replied with a subtle smirk.

"Well, he is the director of one of the world's most powerful spy agencies."

"This...is true," Logan said. "And about all of this, that's for him to tell you. What I'll say is that it goes back to something that should've been dead a long time ago, but unfortunately, some things never die."

"Truer words, my friend. Truer words," Charlie said, as the two men waited in the aftermath of combat for the next phase of chaos to begin.

Chapter 22

John and Amira exited the atrium as the sounds of the battle inside the Ballroom reached them. To their left lay the convention center complex; directly ahead was a grass courtyard with a sidewalk on each side that sloped down to a fountain and the Potomac River; and to the right, the Riverview Ballroom beckoned, a few hundred feet away. The doors facing them bounced repeatedly open like a playing card on a bicycle spokes as people fled the venue.

The gunfire suddenly stopped, and Amira looked at John.

"I just hope Logan got there in time," Amira said.

"It's Logan. He always does. Probably didn't leave any bad guys for us," John replied.

As if in response, Trevor Emerson and Samuel emerged from the building, still holding their pistols. Trevor turned right and fled down the curved sidewalk that ran along the west side of the ballroom to the river. Samuel turned left and ran away from them towards the shopping and dining district.

"You had to open your mouth, didn't you?" Amira said.

"My bad. Which one's yours?" John said.

"I've got the one running towards the river. That's Trevor Emerson, the man who recruited me into the agency and my one-time mentor."

"Roger. I'll take the other guy. Good luck, and be careful, babe." He leaned in, kissed her on the lips, and said, "Happy hunting." He turned and fled down the sidewalk, and she spared two seconds to watch him leave. *God, I love that man.*

A moment later, she broke into a sprint down the left sidewalk that ran to the water, her eyes on Trevor, who'd reached the river view sidewalk. It stretched along the Potomac to the left away from the Gaylord and to the right all the way down to the shops, restaurants, pier, and beyond. He turned left and ran. *He's fast for his age,* Amira thought, relieved he hadn't seen her in pursuit of him.

Bystanders who'd been standing still listening to the gunfire from the Riverview Ballroom and unsure how to react stepped out of his way the moment they saw his gun.

Amira wondered what his destination was, as the river walk ended several hundred yards away before turning back up from the Potomac. *The only thing there is...* And then she knew what his plan was, and she ran harder, trying to close the gap between them.

She reached the river walk moments later and dashed around the corner, barely slowing like a NASCAR driver coming out of a straight-away into a turn. There were still several people between them, but he'd already cleared the last of them and ran harder along the gradual curve to the right where the land jutted out into the Potomac a few hundred yards ahead.

He's going to get there before you. Run FASTER, she heard her father scream inside her head. His voice was a constant in her stream of consciousness since he'd died in her arms, a personification of her moral compass that propelled her. She ran on

137

and focused on her breathing and footing as she pursued the man who'd caused her so much pain.

Trevor had reached a wide, concrete turn-off several hundred feet ahead of her, and he ran up it away from the river.

Just as I predicted, Amira thought, when the sounds of a helicopter reached her ears, an ominous foreboding of things to come. *Bastard always has a plan for every contingency. You know that. But you can still stop him.*

As she gained ground with no more civilians in her way, Trevor reached a chain link fence, pushed open one of the wide fence gates, and ran up the hill. A blue and white civilian helicopter appeared on the horizon and descended towards the area that was Trevor's objective – the full-size Boeing 747 that had been transformed into the Air Force One Experience, a sixty-minute self-guided tour through a replica of the President's official airplane.

This is going to be close, she thought, as she reached the wide concrete turn-off and ran up the hill.

Chapter 23

John ran through the crowd that had formed on the sidewalk outside the Riverview Ballroom as attendees milled about once the gun battle had ended. People parted for him when they saw the Colt 1911 in his right hand, some shouting in fear that he was one of the shooters fleeing the scene. *No time for explanations. Sorry.*

The man Amira had called Samuel was less than a hundred feet away, and he'd reached Waterfront Street, which ran along the side of the Gaylord and its parking lot lobby entrance and sloped down a hill and curved right into the heart of the restaurants and shops.

John ran harder, using his lean form as efficiently as possible, his eyes locked on Samuel. *You'll catch him in ten seconds or less at this pace.*

The man dashed into the street and dodged a red SUV coming up the curve. The driver slammed on the brakes and blew the horn, and John wished he'd struck Samuel and ended the chase. *No such luck.*

Seconds later, a Prince Georges County Police Department blue and silver SUV skidded to a halt in the left lane at the bottom of the hill forty feet in front of the fleeing terrorist. A tall African American officer stepped out, his weapon drawn and tracking Samuel, who kept running.

Samuel never broke stride and veered off towards the door of a restaurant on the right side of the corner. He switched the Glock in his right hand to his left and opened fire blindly to pin the officer down. A stray, lucky round caught the officer flush in the right side of his face, killing him instantly. Samuel never even saw the officer fall, as he burst through the door to Grace's Mandarin Chinese restaurant.

Motherfucker, John thought as he sprinted to where the fallen officer lay, blood trickling from his cheek, his eyes vacant. A chill ran up his spine as he recalled the attack on Amira's father, which included two Calvert County deputies ambushed with non-life-threatening gunshot wounds. *I'm getting tired of law enforcement getting caught in the crossfire of our battles,* he thought disgustedly as he yanked the officer's push-to-talk microphone off his left shoulder. "Officer down outside Grace's Mandarin restaurant at National Harbor. I say again, 'Officer down on Waterfront Street outside Grace's Mandarin. This is John Quick. I'm with the FBI and in pursuit of the subject, a tall, skinny African American dressed in a light grey suit, white shirt, armed. Send additional units immediately. Out."

He dropped the microphone and dashed across the street, ignoring the pedestrians that had scattered away from the gunshots. Task Force Ares technically wasn't part of any agency, but he did have FBI credentials and the blessing of the FBI Director and the president, which was good enough for government work.

John reached the door to Grace's Mandarin and entered in a crouch, moving left inside the foyer into the restaurant. The establishment was a two-story venue whose main dining area was on the second floor with a sweeping view of the Potomac River that curved in alignment with the street. Decorated with traditional Chinese red and gold architecture and statues – complete with upscale cuisine – it was a National Harbor hotspot.

He passed the hostess station as he heard shouts from the second floor, whose balcony overlooked the Koi pond at the bottom of the indoor recirculating waterfall that fell from the second floor along a black granite wall. John dashed to the steps next to the waterfall and crept up them one at a time, his weapon ready and pointed up in case Samuel peeked over the railing of the balcony.

The stairs double backed, and seconds later, his head reached the level of the second floor. A large crash as dishes broke and a cart fell over ahead of him turned his attention to the right along the glass wall and the adjoining tables. Through the legs of tables and chairs, he saw Samuel sprawled on the ground on his stomach, scampering forward as he tried to get up. His hands were empty, which was a relief to John. *Don't need a gunfight in here.*

He holstered the Colt 1911 and moved quickly, recognizing the momentary advantage. John dashed up the last few steps, weaved in between two tables of patrons, and launched himself at Samuel just as the man stood and partially turned. His intent was to incapacitate Samuel without gunfire, as the restaurant was already half full from day shoppers and tourists.

The sidekick he delivered landed squarely on Samuel's ribs, and the skinny man flew sideways into another table, sprawling face-forward onto the assembled meal of the family who sat there, stunned in shock at the sudden confrontation. John moved to incapacitate him when Samuel spun, an empty skewer in his right hand.

John couldn't help himself and stepped back, beckoning with his hands. He was furious that Samuel had just murdered a police officer. *I won't kill him. Just make him hurt. A lot.* "Well, come on then. Let's see what you got, asshole."

Samuel moved as if he'd been electrified, and he jumped forward, the skewer in his right hand and a steak knife appearing in his left. He grinned wickedly, his angular face heightening the expression.

As Samuel closed the distance and lunged in with the knife, John grabbed a heavy rectangular silver serving tray from an empty table and batted the blade away to his left. Acutely aware of the skewer's location, he adjusted his hands and slammed the edge of the tray down on Samuel's left forearm just above the wrist.

The edge struck several nerves, and although not hard enough to break his arm, his hand reflexively opened, and he dropped the steak knife.

Instead of reacting in pain, Samuel twisted his hips and drove the skewer towards John's stomach.

John twisted back to the left, deflecting the attack with the tray. He placed his right foot behind Samuel's and swept it forward to knock the man off-balance, but Samuel was quick, and he lifted his foot up. With nothing to impede his foot, John struck thin air and lurched forward into Samuel as he lost his balance.

Inadvertently having closed the distance, he pressed his shoulder into Samuel's side and drove the man into another table, the tray still a barrier to the skewer.

Fuck this, John thought, and brought his right elbow up and into the side of Samuel's head. The man staggered, and John slammed the edge of the tray into his chest, releasing it after the impact. He reached forward with both hands and grabbed Samuel's right wrist, intent on smashing his arm against a table.

Samuel recognized his intent, and he did the only thing he could think to prevent it – he drove his legs forward, pushing the two men towards the railing fifteen feet away.

"Mother...fucker," John said with anger. He was in a pure battle rage and desperately wanted to defeat the evil man in his grasp. "You want to go for a ride? Fine. *Let's go.*"

John started running *with* Samuel, accelerating their approach towards the red decorated railing.

Samuel glanced at his pursuer's face and saw only resolve and fury, and he realized he'd started something he couldn't stop. *This man is going to kill me.*

The rage at the officer's murder on the street fueled John, and he drove his legs harder, the two men gaining speed. Less than two feet from the railing, John released Samuel's wrist with his right hand and grabbed him at the right armpit. He twisted to the left and braced his legs for the impact. Their momentum carried him forward, but John pulled upward with all his strength as the two collided with the railing. His lower body slammed into the thick, metal panel, and he prayed it held as he yanked and pushed Samuel over the top.

Samuel disappeared, and John dropped down further, trying to lower his center of gravity. He felt the panel railing sway but hold.

He heard a splash below, and thought, *Hope that hurt like hell,* wondering which part of the Koi pond he'd hit.

There was a second splash, and John felt a moment of panic. *No way.* He stood up and glanced over the railing just in time to see Samuel dash out the door, the skewer sticking out of his upper left shoulder.

Good God, John thought as he moved towards the steps to continue the pursuit. *This guy won't quit.*

Chapter 24

The helicopter had already landed by the time Amira ran through the chain-link fence gate and up the hill. A Bell 505, the smallest utility helicopter in Bell's production line, the blue and white chopper sat on the pavement thirty yards away from the nose of the Air Force One replica as Trevor Emerson stepped into the open cabin on the passenger side. A man and a woman stood near the ticket booth at the bottom of the drivable passenger stairs that led up to the hatch of the plane. The downdraft of the rotor wash whipped around them, and they huddled together in the waning daylight.

Amira ran as hard as she could towards the helicopter, intent on maximizing her only chance to prevent Trevor Emerson from escaping justice. Her eyes were glued to the cockpit, but she wasn't fixed on Trevor. *The pilot's the only way.* She didn't know who the man was, his history, what family he had. All that mattered was that he'd agreed to act as a get-away pilot for a traitor, and that fact alone sealed his fate.

As she grew closer, the helicopter lifted into the air as Trevor took the co-pilot's chair on the right and watched Amira through the plexiglass. She was less than thirty feet away when she stopped and raised the SIGSAUER P229 9mm pistol and trained it on the pilot, who was focused on a clean takeoff so close to the Air Force One Experience. The helicopter continued to climb, but not quickly enough. Even though her sights were placed on the upper body of the pilot, she saw the look of fear appear on the face of Trevor and was pleased at the reaction. *Time to test my aim.* She pulled the trigger slowly, and the accurate 9mm pistol bucked in her hand.

A spiderweb appeared in the cockpit glass where the pilot's face had been, and Amira pulled the trigger again. More holes appeared in a perfect grouping. She waited for a response, but the helicopter hung suspended in the air, thirty-five feet above the pavement. *Did I miss?*

The nose of the helicopter suddenly lurched and tilted forward as if tipping over, its nose pointed to the ground. The two people near the ticket booth were jarred from their amazement, and they turned and fled under the left wing of the Boeing 747 away from the helicopter.

The helicopter shot forward and down, and Amira realized her aim had been true – she'd struck the pilot, and he'd pushed the cyclic flight stick forward and turned the throttle, which both dipped the nose and accelerated the revolutions per minute of the rotors. The Bell 505 shot forward directly towards the upper cockpit area of the Air Force One replica.

Oh no, Amira thought, and turned away from the inevitable.

In a tremendous roar that seemed to rip the world apart, the rotors of the Bell 505 slashed into the aluminum skin of the 747, tearing chunks of the shell away in pieces that flew in all directions, skipping across the pavement. The bird dug into the airplane, burrowing itself deeper as its engine disintegrated and the rotors broke apart, including a huge piece that tore a chunk of concrete three feet away from Amira's head as she lay prone on the pavement, her hands over her head in defensive but useless protection. And then the world went silent, the unfolding destruction over.

Amira looked back in awe at the 747 and the Bell 505 that now lay partially buried within the nose of the plane, its cockpit swallowed whole. Smoke rose from the ruined engine on top of the helicopter, but there were no flames. *That's one small mercy. But there's still one last thing to do.*

Amira strode purposefully towards the stairs, which had escaped the destruction. She had to confirm that Trevor Emerson was dead or alive. The day could not end without it.

Chapter 25

John cringed in pain as he took the steps two at a time, his back throbbing from where he'd crashed into the railing. He hit the ground floor, ran past the hostess station, and exited the same way he'd entered less than ninety seconds before. There was blood on the sidewalk, and the skewer lay discarded. *If nothing else, I hope the bastard dies of some kind of foodborne illness,* he thought wishfully.

He looked in both directions and heard shouts from around the curve to the right. He broke into a run, the pain in his back transitioning from the stabbing phase to the dull, throbbing phase, relieved at the slight improvement.

He rounded the corner and spotted Samuel less than a block away, crossing the street in a sprint in front of a Starbucks. *Come on, man. Why do you have to make this so hard?*

John ignored the pain, tapped into his reserves, and ran faster, his eyes tracking Samuel. While the skinny African was fast, John was faster, and he'd already reached the midpoint of the block when Samuel disappeared to the left around the corner.

John knew there was no chance Samuel could escape, but he also knew the man's fight-or-flight mode was fully engaged, and there was no shutting it off until he'd been caught. John had participated in too many chases like this one, and just like high-speed police pursuits, they usually ended only one way – with dramatic destruction and the suspect in custody or dead. *And it's your job to make sure no one else gets hurt.*

John reached the Starbucks on the corner to his left and kept running. National Plaza Street curved to the right along the water, with the Redstone American Grill restaurant on the left. Just past the restaurant was the entrance to the pier, which was where Samuel was when a second police vehicle squealed to a stop in the middle of the street. Unarmed, Samuel did the only thing a desperate man could do – he bolted left down the pier.

Seconds later, John reached the same spot and screamed to the female African American Prince Georges County deputy who'd emerged from the SUV, "I'm FBI! I got this. Get to the Grace's Mandarin to your fallen officer."

He didn't wait for a response and ran up the pier, passing the enormous sand playground that contained a silver head and limbs sticking out from the sand, as if a giant were emerging from the ground. Known as The Awakening, it was another sight to behold at the National Harbor on a normal day that didn't involve gunfire and mayhem.

The pier was several hundred feet long and ended in one of the biggest attractions in the area – the Capital Wheel, a one-hundred-and-eighty-foot-tall Ferris wheel that provided views of the Potomac, Alexandria, the National Monument, the Capitol, and even the National Cathedral far away up the hill in northwest DC.

This late in the afternoon so close to dusk, there was a lull of pedestrians on the pier, and both men ran around them like football players conducting cone drills.

John was within twenty yards of Samuel when the fleeing man reached the end of the pier and the enormous wheel above him. He shouted, "Just stop for God's sakes! There's nowhere left to run. I won't shoot you if you surrender." His Kimber was trained on Samuel's back, but the big gondolas kept spinning behind him, and he didn't want to risk striking one.

Samuel turned as the few pedestrians in the area scattered at the appearance of the two men. John's peripheral vision caught a teenaged couple pull out cell phones and begin recording. *Perfect. Just what I need. To be on Tik Tok.*

"You're right, but it doesn't matter. This country has no place for me. I'd rather die than spend time in one of your prisons."

"Well, I know what the prisons are like in Sudan," John replied, recalling what Logan and Cole Matthews had told him about the black site prison they'd broken out of on their operation in Sudan. "And ours make yours look like wealthy country clubs. You killed a police officer back there, and no matter what happens, you're going to pay for it. Your only hope is to stop running and get on the ground. *Now.*"

Samuel contemplated his fate, and he knew that the man spoke the truth. But he also didn't care. His war had ended with South Sudan's independence. Asim's first cousin, he'd already been in America working as a taxi driver in DC when Omar had approached him months ago with an opportunity for vengeance. He'd tired of feeling like a cliché, a foreigner driving a cab in a rich country's capital. The amount of money Omar had offered would have provided him a comfortable life until the end of his years, but that was not to be, and he knew it. But he also knew he'd rather die on his own terms than surrender on his knees in front of this American. *I can die with honor,* he thought, and responded with one resolute word: "No." He turned and ran up the steps that led to the loading platform of the gondolas.

"I knew this wasn't going to be easy," John muttered to himself as he reached the steps just as Samuel disappeared on the back side of the stairs. John bounded up the steps, reached the top, and leapt over a railing that divided the wide steps into multiple boarding lanes that led back down to the platform.

"Hey! What are you doing?" a white male in his thirties, one of the Capital Wheel operators, exclaimed more in surprise than fear at the appearance of the skinny black man with a bloody white shirt.

The operator stepped in front of Samuel, even as John clambered down the steps. He looked past Samuel at John, saw the pistol and FBI badge dangling from his neck, and said, "What the hell?"

Samuel punched the man in the face, stepped forward, and delivered a violent push that sent the staggered man flying across the platform. He landed on his haunches and lay back, dazed at the violent attack.

The only good thing about the assault was that it provided John the extra seconds he needed to holster his Colt 1911 and close the distance to Samuel. His prey heard his approach above the mechanical hum of the Ferris wheel's four fifty-horsepower engines, and he turned his head just as John crashed into his back and sent the skinny man flying to his knees.

Multiple white steel canopies with white, opaque panels covered the space, creating shifting shadows in the fading daylight as the gondolas kept slowly moving down across the platform and back into the air.

"You," John said to the fallen operator. "Get up and get out of here. *Move.*" The command shook the man back to reality, and he rose, moving slowly to the steps, holding his jaw where he'd been struck.

When the operator was out of sight, John stood still and waited for Samuel to recover. The man turned to face him, straightening up from the blow John had just delivered.

"Last chance. I won't ask again."

Samuel only smiled in a weird, bitter way, as if laughing at himself. "You are correct. At some point, we all run out of chances."

Samuel rushed forward and threw a flurry of punches aimed at John's head. John slipped and batted them away, as he found himself against one of the white steel girders supporting a canopy. Samuel suddenly turned to his left and swept his right leg up in a smooth roundhouse kick. John sidestepped it to his left and pushed Samuel's shoe harder, forcing it to strike the steel girder.

Samuel grunted in pain and brought his leg back to the platform.

"That had to hurt, Samuel. Sure sounded like it. You want to keep doing this, or can we call it a day?"

"You know my name," Samuel said, pursing his lips. "Very well. What's yours?"

"John, and that's all you're going to get from me until you stop fighting."

Samuel shrugged, and instead, rushed forward, trying to tackle John, who brought both elbows down on the man's upper back.

Playtime's over, John. End this, Amira's voice sounded calmly in his head.

John twisted to his left and raised a knee into the bent-over Samuel's midsection. He repeated the move two more times until he felt the man go slack in his arms. He stepped to his right and flung the man away, sending him to the platform in a heap of battered bones.

He moved closer to restrain Samuel when the fallen man somehow rose to his feet and turned to face John one last time. In his right hand was a small black knife with a curved tip and serrated back. He stared at John, and then he motioned with his left hand for John to come to him. It was the act of a man who wanted one last opportunity to prove himself before his conqueror.

153

For the briefest of moments, John considered the challenge, but then he thought of Amira, and rational discourse took control in his head. *I'm too old for this shit.*

In a blinding move, he drew his Kimber and fired a .45-caliber slug that struck Samuel in the upper right leg, shattering his femur. The man shrieked in pain and collapsed backwards through the opening in the railing for passengers to load and unload the gondolas.

John recognized what was coming, but there was nothing he could do to stop it. By trying to preserve Samuel's life, albeit with a severe wound to his leg, he'd inadvertently doomed him to death. It was like watching a horrific car accident in excruciating slow motion.

Samuel howled in pain as the fifteen-hundred-pound, climate-controlled gondola descended on to the platform with less than ten inches of clearance below the massive carriage. He sensed the presence of the car and turned to his left, just in time to see the black bottom of the car smash into his face, breaking his nose and left cheekbone. His head twisted to the right as the car traveled over his body, rolling and breaking it inch by inch as it slowly worked its way across him. He screamed in agony, but his cry was cut short as his head was pinned next to his shoulder and the carriage snapped his neck with a loud *crack* that made John wince.

The car cleared the body, and John stepped forward and grabbed Samuel's legs. He pulled the dead man clear of the opening, and Samuel's eyes stared up accusingly from a head that had been internally and bloodlessly decapitated.

John stared down at the man, but he felt no sympathy for the cop killer who lay dead before him. "You brought this on yourself. No one else," he whispered, and turned away to find the wounded operator to turn off the Wheel. Whatever passengers were left onboard were about to find out that they'd paid for a ride that included homicide as an added attraction.

Chapter 26

Amira stepped off the mobile staircase and into a hellish landscape of twisted metal, leaking fluids, and dark shadows. Immediately to her left was the nose of the plane where the museum had reconstructed the presidential sleeping quarters. She'd seen pictures of it in the press coverage that had announced the Air Force One Experience – two blue-blanketed beds, one on each side of the nose angling in towards each other, wood paneling shelves, a wooden chair, and even a large desk at the foot of the bed on the starboard side of the plane. But that picture had been wiped away, replaced with something ripped from a disaster movie.

With dusk approaching, the presidential quarters were shrouded in darkness. The bulbous glass of the cockpit stretched across the space, a black glossy reflection that touched each bed as if the mechanical beast slumbered upon them. There was a gap where the open compartment of the helicopter intersected with the skin of the plane, but all she saw was darkness, taunting her with hidden threats. Overhead, chunks of the airplane's skin had been torn from the frame by the rotors as if a giant clawed beast had swiped at the nose. The desk had been toppled over and amazingly stood on its left end as if at attention, a deep crack running down the middle of the bottom of the desk. Hissing and popping noises rose from the helicopter's ruined engine, and the pungent odor of hydraulic fluid and aviation kerosene filled the space. She realized the cockpit glistened because of the fluids leaking down it like a slow-moving lava lamp.

She held her pistol close to her chest, ready to extend and fire at the first moving object. *Here we go.* She took a step forward so she could peer into the cockpit and determine if Trevor was trapped inside with the pilot. Part of her hoped he'd died in the accident, but either way, she had to know for certain. She took a second step towards the plexiglass when she sensed movement from her right, and she instinctively sidestepped to the left as the axe sailed by her right arm, missing by inches.

Bastard, she thought as she shot out her arms to neutralize Trevor, whose face was a red mask from the lateral gash he'd sustained above his forehead when he'd struck the windshield in the crash. He wielded a crash axe constructed of a titanium handle, stainless-steel blade, and a stainless-steel pike. Lightweight, it had gaps in the handle and looked like it had been constructed out of metallic bones and belonged in the hands of a Viking, not a former CIA employee. Trevor brought the pike end of the savage-looking weapon back up and knocked Amira's pistol away as the pointed pike buried itself in her forearm.

The weapon discharged, a deafening sound in the enclosed space, and she dropped it from the pain that shot up her arm. She grunted through the white hot agony as Trevor pulled the weapon free from her arm. He swung the axe down and backwards in a wide circle as he tried to bring it down on top of Amira, but she reached up with her fully functional left arm and grabbed the handle just above his right hand, stopping the axe at its apex. While her right hand might have dropped her pistol reflexively, the hand still worked, and she balled it into a fist and smashed it into Trevor's face.

Trevor brought his left arm up to defend against the blows, but several punches landed, dazing him.

Amira sensed the momentary weakness and slammed his right hand against the cockpit plexiglass. She delivered a knee to his left side and felt his body weaken, even though he still held the axe handle. She slammed his hand one more time against the Plexiglass and held it in place as she punched the underside of his right wrist as hard as she could. The result was instantaneous, and his hand reflexively opened, releasing its grip on the axe.

The axe fell, and she caught it in her left hand, ending its freefall. She spun like the ballet dancer that she once was in a perfect pirouette, pike end of the axe flashing around her in a flat arc.

Trevor sensed the motion and dropped down into a crouch, and the pike sailed over his head and buried itself into the Plexiglass of the cockpit.

Amira yanked on the axe, and the pike freed itself, tearing a chunk of Plexiglass away.

Trevor launched a sharp uppercut, but Amira moved her head, partially slipping it. The force of the punch was still enough to send pain shooting along her left jawline, but she ignored it and brought the end of the axe handle straight down into the middle of his back. While it wasn't sharp enough to pierce his body, the chisel and wire-cutter handle shot pain up the middle of his back, and he dropped to his knees. She struck him again, and he fell face-down on to the yellowish-beige carpet, which was soaked from the leaking hydraulic fluid and aviation kerosene.

Time for the killing blow, Amira thought, tossed the axe from her left hand to right, and raised her arm high over her head. She paused for the briefest of moments as memories of her experiences with her mentor, the man who'd recruited her into the shadowy world of the CIA, flickered through her mind like images in a child's View Master. She still remembered verbatim the first conversation she'd had with him, how he'd seen into her unlike any person she'd met before, had known what she was, even before she fully realized it. As much as she despised the traitor who lay at her feet, she was grateful for the patriot and man that he'd once been. She was torn, and she wavered between action and inaction for the first time in her life, and then she recognized it for what it was – the uneasy feeling of doubt. The epiphany struck her harder than any blow Trevor had landed. *But what will you do, now? Kill or capture. It's what it always comes down to, and it always will.* She wasn't sure, and she faltered, acutely aware that time was slipping away like a dark, endless tide.

A loud groan suddenly built into a roar, and Amira recognized the impending catastrophe before it happened. She leapt towards the opening to the presidential quarters as the beds exploded under the weight of the ruined helicopter. The cockpit lurched forward further into the airplane, the Plexiglass cockpit landing on the lower back of Trevor Emerson, pinning him to the carpet like a bug on display. He was facedown, his arms and legs sticking out from under each side of the cockpit. He screamed in pain and looked up at Amira, tilting his head as high as it would go. A dull flicker appeared from above the cockpit, blossoming into a flame that licked at the cockpit's surface.

"Please," Trevor implored, panicked eyes pleading for mercy. "Help me."

Amira stared down at her former mentor and then looked around the ruined display. "I just did. Because of the man you once were, I held my hand from driving this axe into the back of your head. But I guess fate judged you differently," she said, sweeping her arms across the room. "You got yourself into this mess. If you can get yourself out, you'll still go to prison for the rest of your life. But I'll give you that chance, for old time's sake, for the man you used to be, not the ruined one before me." Amira tossed the axe on the carpet and picked up her pistol, which lay at her feet. She holstered the weapon, and said, "Goodbye, Trevor."

She walked out of the display as the fire grew in intensity, ignoring the pleas and screams behind her, and exited the airplane with a clear conscience. *I bet they won't put that on the Air Force One Experience,* she heard John's voice quip inside her head and smiled at her lover's imagined voice.

Amira walked a safe distance away and sat on the pavement as the fire engulfed the plane, a flaming beacon for all to witness as

160

night fell across the National Harbor. Just as she'd done on the night she'd survived the attack at the University of Maryland, she sat in silence and relished the victory in the aftermath of the battle.

You won again, and it feels good because you were on the right side. This is who you are and always will be. A warrior. To the end.

She smiled, content in the truth of that knowledge, the glow of the flames heightening her intense beauty as the fire raged around her.

Epilogue

McLean, Virginia
Two Weeks Later
1425 EST

Beth Cathey was exhausted from the stress of the past few weeks, wondering when the agency's counterintelligence division or security personnel would show up with questions. She felt trapped, her heart hammering in her chest every minute of every day she'd been at work at Langley since the attack at the National Harbor. But as the days ticked by, the panic slowly subsided from a raging storm threatening to paralyze her to a subdued presence, and she began to think they didn't know. She wouldn't have been the first insider threat the agency had failed to uncover. The number of leaks over the past several years had piled up so quickly it was impossible to keep up with the flow of compromised information.

She'd tried to contact Amira, but her calls had gone unreturned, only adding to her sense of impending doom.

Beth opened the front door of her three-level town home and glanced at her watch as the alarm beeped. She had a few minutes to change into something other than her agency attire – a form-fitting dark grey business suit and white shirt – before she picked up Alexa.

She walked across the small foyer, entered the disarm code on her alarm system, and placed her keys on a small console table. She caught a glimpse of herself in the mirror above the table.

162

Normally, a very attractive brunette with chestnut brown hair that hung below her shoulders – although she kept it in a neat ponytail for work – and sharp, chiseled features, she looked tired with lines on her face she hadn't noticed before. *It's taking its toll on you and finally showing.*

The main floor of the town home was wide open, with her family room on the left, which emptied into a large kitchen and then a three-story bump-out with a sunroom. The family room had been decorated for Christmas, and the artificial tree stood on the left side near the wall, waiting for Alexa to open the presents Beth would place there on the Big Day. A staircase to her right led upstairs, and just past the console table, another set of stairs led to the basement. Beyond the basement stairs was a large dining area on the right half of the kitchen that led to the outdoor deck. Due to the staircases, the table was just out of view, which was why she didn't see Amira Cerone sitting at the table, holding a suppressed SIGSAUER P229 9mm pistol pointed at her chest.

Dressed in jeans, a deep red sweater, and a dark navy overcoat, she blended in well with the upscale townhome community. "It's a nice place you have, Beth. Truly."

Beth studied her friend, and said, "Thanks. I spend most of my income on this and Alexa's daycare."

"We know," Amira replied.

Beth nodded at the plural form of the subject. *The proverbial gig is up.* "Do you want a cup of coffee? I need one…if that's okay."

"It is, and then I need you to sit down so we can talk."

Beth walked over to the Nespresso machine, turned it on, inserted a pod, and turned back to Amira as the creamy coffee brewed. "You know I have to pick up Alexa in forty-five minutes from day care, right?"

"We know. Don't worry. She'll be fine," Amira said.

Not "You'll be fine," but "She'll be fine." This isn't good. The panic was once again full-blown, and she forced herself to remain calm as her world slowly crashed down upon her. She took her mug and joined Amira at the table.

"I just need to know why," Amira said. "That's all."

Beth's face broke into a mask of shame and sorrow at what she'd done to her friend and ally. She'd considered what she'd say to Amira if the moment ever arose, and here it was, reflecting her own guilt and pain in the form of her friend. She composed herself quickly, looked Amira in the eyes, and said, "They took Alexa two days before we had lunch. I don't know how, but they knew I'd reached out to you. When I first did, that was truly because I was worried about you, but they changed that. They told me to get you to that lunch at that time and place. They told me that if I didn't, they'd kill Alexa." She paused, the thought of her daughter dead stifling her ability to speak. "When they took her, they told her I had to go out of town on business, but they let me talk to her. I said her regular sitter was sick and that the people with her would take care of her and that I'd see her in a few days. And God bless her, she believed me. It was awful, but they said any outside involvement would end in her death."

"Why didn't you come to me for help? Believe me when I tell you the people I work with could've helped," Amira said.

"Amira, I believed them, completely. I didn't know it was Trevor at the time. I only found out about that after you killed him. I have to say this, and God help me, but I'd have done it again. I'm so sorry, but I'd do *anything* for my daughter. As a parent – and you'll learn this someday if you have kids – my only job is to keep Alexa safe from the horrors of the world, raise her the best that I can as a single mom, and prepare her for the world when it's her time to go out into it. And by setting up that lunch, I protected her one more time. I'm sorry, but it's the awful truth."

Amira sat in silence, contemplating every word Beth spoke, knowing the conviction behind them and the truth that underpinned them. *She's just a mom protecting her family. And remember, it was your actions in Sudan that started this chain of events. If anything, you pulled her into this, not the other way around.* The pang of guilt she felt at that realization had been eating away at her. Had she not killed Asim and left Omar alive, none of this would've happened. *I killed the wrong man.* That was the truth. Based on what Nafisa had said about her husband just before she died, he hadn't been like Omar. He wouldn't have sought vengeance the way Omar had. He'd been a good man, even under the rebel disguise, and she'd killed him. *So much pain and loss.* Trevor had been right about one thing – the world never changed. The people,

165

the missions, the deaths, they all changed, but not the struggle between the West and the rest of the world. It was endless.

"I believe you," Amira said. "And I'm sorry you got pulled into this. It goes back to an operation I did in South Sudan before I ended up where I am now. But that's all I can tell you. More importantly, I believe you when you say you did what you did to protect Alexa, and I can't fault you for that. You're not the first parent forced into a horrific situation, and you won't be the last. That's why you're still breathing, because Alexa needs a mother, especially in this world." The implication was clear – if she'd wanted, she could've killed Beth, and no one would've batted an eye. And Beth knew it.

Amira also knew that Beth's ex-husband, a banker, had left when Alexa was one and moved to California to remarry a twenty-five-year-old spin instructor. It had been the worst form of a cliché imaginable for Beth when it had happened, and she'd dedicated herself to providing Alexa everything she needed.

"But there are no free passes, Beth. And I need you to understand and accept that. It looks like the Chinese may ultimately have been behind this attack, and if so, trust me when I tell you my friends and I will find out. But that fight is for another day." She paused, like a judge about to render a sentence. "So here's the deal, with the blessing of Director Tooney, a personal friend of mine: effectively immediately, you are no longer an employee of the CIA. Your badge access was revoked within minutes of your departure today. Additionally, you will never hold a position or a clearance in any government agency ever again. Your time as a federal employee is over, permanently." Amira watched as each word struck her friend like a blow, causing Beth to wince as her sentence was read aloud. "Having said that, the agency will provide a reference for you if you need one in the future. You were an outstanding employee before this, but like I said, some things can't be undone, and this is one of them. Do you understand everything I just told you, Beth?"

For Beth, the gates of her guilt broke apart, and a torrent of relief rushed through her. Tears formed in her eyes, and when she finally spoke, it was with sincere gratitude. "Thank you. And Amira, I'm sorry. For all of it."

"So am I," Amira said, and stood up, unscrewing the suppressor and holstering the pistol under her coat and placing the suppressor in a deep coat pocket, the need for the threat of violence over. "One last thing, Beth, the two hundred and fifty thousand dollars they gave you, we know about that."

"I figured. It showed up in my account after they returned Alexa. I had no idea. They said it was to guarantee my silence because it made it look like I'd been paid off. I honestly didn't know what I was going to do with it."

"Well, my suggestion is that you use it to raise Alexa. And if I were you, I'd go back to the Midwest, maybe use that Masters in Elementary Education and become a teacher. But regardless, your time in this world of ours is over." She walked behind Beth and placed her left hand on her friend's right shoulder. "You won't ever see me again. Goodbye, Beth," Amira said, squeezed her friend's shoulder, and walked out of the town home into the cold December day.

She inhaled deeply, the smell of the crisp air intoxicating after the emotional goodbye inside. *You did the right thing. You gave her a second chance, and she knows it. You have to let everything else go. You made a choice in Sudan, and you can't take it back. You can learn from it and move forward, or you can let it pull you under,* her father's voice told her. *But that's not who you are, Princess. You're a warrior, my Amira,* her father's love once again comforting her. *I miss you, Daddy. I love you so much.*

She pulled out her iPhone and called John. "It's done."

"Good," he said, absent of his typical sarcasm. "Are you coming home?"

She smiled for no one to see. "You're there, aren't you?"

"You know it, babe," John replied casually.

"Then that's where home is. I love you, John Quick. I'll see you soon," and disconnected the phone.

The weather called for a snowstorm with more than eighteen inches, which would paralyze a city like Washington DC, which usually reacted chaotically over three to four inches. The upside was that she'd be socked in with John in their loft apartment in Fall's Church, and the thought left her smiling as she walked to the black Ford Explorer.

The world would continue to wobble on its axis, violently at times, but she and John had each other, which was all they could ask for. Their today was enough for each of them, as no one was ever promised a tomorrow.

Author's Note

Dear Friends, Fans, & Readers,

Over the years of the Logan West series, I've received more fan letters and emails about Amira since I introduced her in my second thriller, OATH OF HONOR. She has been one of my most-cherished characters to develop, and her story arc has been filled with love, heartbreak, loss, and resolve, especially after the events of RULES OF WAR and the death of her father. I'd always planned to write her origin story and revisit her past, including her mission in Sudan that I referenced when you first meet her in OATH. And now, for a variety of reasons, the timing seemed perfect, and I wrote this story from December 2020 to January 2021.

The goals of this story are, first and foremost, to entertain; to elicit an emotional response; to delve deeper into the origins of Amira's character; and to draw you further into the world of Logan West. I hope you love it as much as I loved writing it. I have to admit, the scene in Sudan is one of the favorite things I've penned. It's just chilling and terrifying when you really envision yourself in that scene.

As for what comes next in the world of Logan West, I honestly don't know. Since I've been in this business and signed my first book deal in 2014, I've often been accused of being too honest, too direct, and too open, but as a recovering alcoholic and former Marine, I truly don't know how to be any other way. As much as people in this business want me to change – and they've tried; believe me – I won't. It's just not in my nature. I will succeed or fail on my own merits, and like the alien hunter says at the end of PREDATOR, "I am what I am." And in that vein, I have to tell you that after four Logan West books, I amicably left Simon & Schuster.

As you likely know, THE NEIGHBORHOOD, my next major novel, a standalone about a gated community that comes under siege one night by an assault force looking for something and turns into a modern take on a spy thriller with atypical characters, comes out from Blackstone Publishing in 2022. I actually finished that novel early last year, which was why I had the time to write AMIRA. And while AMIRA is as polished as any of my thrillers (fun fact: I love editing, for real), I'm self-publishing this one through Amazon. It gives me the flexibility to do it exactly the way I wanted and deliver a high-quality product at a greatly reduced price. Having said that, to write a full-length Logan West thriller (and I've had a great story line in my head for two years, and it's still current), AMIRA will have to do well. That is just the brutal truth of this business.

No matter what you may think of publishing, it is infinitely harder than you can imagine, with roadblocks created at every junction and business models that literally operate backwards. I was naïve when I started in this business, but a few years beat that naivete right out of me like Amira beat Omar. Having said that, no matter where my writing takes me, I want to return to the universe of Logan West at some point.

And with that, I wish you all well. I pray you made it through 2020 safe and healthy, and I pray life will return to some sort of normalcy as soon as possible. I am forever in your debt, for without you, there is no Amira Cerone, and there is no wonderful world of Logan West. Onward.

About The Author

Matthew Betley is a former Marine officer of ten years. His experience includes deployments to Djibouti after September 11, and to Iraq prior to The Surge. A New Jersey native who grew up in Cincinnati, he graduated from Miami University in Oxford, Ohio, with a BA in psychology and minors in political science and sociology. Most importantly, Matt is a recovering alcoholic 12 years sober and an advocate for victims of toxic burn pit exposure from deployments to Iraq, Afghanistan, and other bases around the world.

Made in the USA
Monee, IL
10 March 2023

9f9189d3-b5b7-4511-bb1f-713263224323R01